H

MW00882355

A Son's Journey Home

A Novel

Revised and Expanded

From the author of *Waiting on Zapote Street*,
winner of the Latino Books Into Movies Award,
Drama TV Series category

Betty Viamontes

Havana: A Son's Journey Home

Published in the United States by Zapote Street Books, LLC, Tampa, Florida

This book is a work of fiction. Characters, names, places, events, incidents, and businesses are either a product of the author's imagination or used fictitiously. Any resemblance to actual locales or events, or to any persons, living or dead, is entirely coincidental.

ISBN: 978-1-723867668

Printed in the United States of America

I dedicate this book to—

My mother, my beacon of light even after her death.

My beloved husband, for supporting my community involvement and writing career, for being the love of my life and my best friend.

My loyal readers, for reading my books, telling others about them, taking the time to write reviews on Amazon and Goodreads, and encouraging me to keep writing.

Our beloved Alfredo Portomeñe, a good father, son, grandfather, and cousin. Someone who exemplified the word love and left us too soon.

The members of all the book clubs who so kindly have chosen to read *Waiting on Zapote Street*, *The Dance of the Rose*, and *Candela's Secrets and Other Havana Stories*.

.

CHAPTER 1

OVER THE LAST FEW WEEKS, the seventeen-year-old, Rodolfo Fernandez, has been filled with fears. Fear of flying. Fear of a new city. Fear of a new language and culture. On this day, his fear of dying takes center stage. He is on the second leg of his trip from Madrid—where he had lived with his aunt and uncle for over a year—and as the Boeing 727 begins its descent into Miami International Airport, he's unsettled by turbulence.

Thoughts of an aircraft of the same model flying from Frankfurt to London—and crashing during the landing—cast a chill through him. His hands turn clammy as he senses a tight feeling in his stomach. A few days before, he and his relatives in Madrid had watched the aftermath of the accident during the evening news. He couldn't sleep well for several nights, thinking of his upcoming trip.

His brown eyes search for signs of alarmed passengers. No one seems concerned, so he inhales and returns the book he had been reading,

Chapter 1

One Hundred Years of Solitude, to his leather bag. He rubs his hands over his face while the bumpy ride increases his pulse. Sitting in a middle seat on Row 24, surrounded by strangers, and thinking he might die in that flight, he doesn't understand why some people enjoy flying for a living. His uncle in Madrid is one of them. Always traveling by plane to various cities in Europe, selling pharmaceuticals. Rodolfo wouldn't want a job where he has to be stuck inside a metal gadget in the sky, thousands of meters above earth, several hours a week. To give up control of one's short time on earth, to whomever happens to be sitting in the cockpit, sounds ludicrous to him. He closes his eyes and holds on to the arm rests, as if doing so could protect him from the ideas in his head. Moments later, he feels a slight touch on his left hand. His eyes open.

"Would you like a mint?" the female passenger next to him asks him.

"No, thank you," he replies.

She smiles at him with her recently-colored pink lips.

"No need to worry," she says. "This turbulence is normal."

But nothing she can tell him will calm him as he imagines the wreckage of the aircraft and the passengers' belongings scattered near the scene of the accident. Then he decides to concentrate on his breathing. In… out… in… out.

The passenger next to him reminds him of his mother, about the same age, talkative and maternal like her, particularly after she'd learned earlier in the flight he was flying alone. From that moment forward, when the cart passed by, she nudged him to make sure he didn't miss any food or drinks—just like his mother would've done. His mind drifts to the last time he saw her, back in Havana, over a year ago.

**

"Hurry please!" his mother said with a hasty voice, turning her head in his direction. He gave her an empty, unsympathetic look and continued to walk with unwilling steps. Inside her mind, her determination to set him free and reluctance to let him go fought an endless war.

"Rodolfo, do *not* test my patience," she added and jerked the teen's arm. "We're almost out of time."

She, Ana Romero, began to run with short strides, pulling him by his arm, her black eyes now focused somewhere in the distance.

Days later she would tell him, in letters or telephone conversations, that as many times as she'd imagined that day, it was far worse. Her chest felt tight and her muscles tensed.

"This is the right thing to do," she kept telling herself.

Her form-fitting red dress, sleeveless and elegant, accentuated her curves. For as long as he could remember, his mother dressed to impress, even after the triumph of the revolution, but especially on the day of his trip. Her black heels echoed on the granite floor of Rancho Boyeros Airport, and the subtle scent of her flowery perfume lingered in the air as she walked. A black leather bag, matching the color of her hair, hung from her shoulder, while the blue suitcase she carried swung like a pendulum.

Rodolfo looked younger than his age, with his brown hair, parted to one side by his mother before he left the house—against his wishes—and his smooth face with early signs of a mustache. He squinted at her as he followed her. "Invisible." That word popped into his head. That was how she made him feel. She had not asked him for his opinion about this trip; or he would have told her that his life was in Cuba, with his girlfriend, Susana—a month younger than him. He would've told her he preferred to stay at the place he considered home, with his family and friends. He wanted nothing else. Years later, he would look back to this day in a very different way, not through the lenses of a teenager.

The night before, when he and Susana walked on Santos Suárez Park holding hands, he didn't tell her he was leaving. His mother had ordered him to keep his imminent departure a secret to avoid attracting the attention of gossipers and government sympathizers. She said if he didn't, he would put the family at risk.

That evening, when he kissed Susana goodbye, he held her hand, thinking it would be the last time. She wore a flowing white dress, sleeveless; her thin arms wrapped around him while her black long hair danced in the tropical breeze. She was his first love, but in his affection for her, pity had found a home. Her father had been shot by Castro's firing squad when she was eight years old, and now he was about to break her heart again.

As Rodolfo dashed through the airport, his white, long-sleeved shirt—rolled up to his elbows—revealed his thin arms and a scar on top of his right hand. It was around two inches in diameter, from the time his mother's pressure cooker blew up and sprayed scalding water all over the tiny kitchen. The navy pants his aunt had sent him from Spain looked big on him, but a belt held them in place.

"Why do we have to keep running, Mamá?" Rodolfo asked, stomping his feet on the ground. "Slow down!"

Mortified, she stopped for a moment, turned her face towards him, and beckoned him with her index finger to get closer. He obeyed, narrowing the space between them.

"I don't want you to miss the flight!" she spoke between her teeth, opening her eyes wide. "Hurry. We need to buy a ticket."

Before she jerked him by his arm again, she gave him a look he knew too well—determined, unyielding, one that never failed to get his attention, and in this case, made him realize that testing her patience wouldn't accomplish anything, other than, perhaps, provoking her pinches.

Mother and child started to run again, as drops of perspiration formed on her brow. Ahead, beyond the crowd, the view of the ticket counter seemed to relax the anxiety contorting her expression. Once in front of it, she dropped the luggage on the floor and let go of her son's hand to reach inside her purse. Frantically, she took some money out of her wallet.

"One-way ticket to Madrid, please," she said without looking at the plump, bald-headed male clerk.

"Sorry, comrade. The last flight to Madrid is full. It leaves in less than an hour."

"But you don't understand!" she said, raising her voice. "My son needs to get on this flight. He *can't* stay here."

Adjusting his glasses, he gave her a blank stare.

"Please, sir," she said in a kinder, calmer tone, placing her hand over his. "He'll turn sixteen tomorrow. He *has* to leave!"

"I can't help you, comrade," the clerk said, retrieving his hand. Then, with a jeering laughter, he added: "Besides, stop worrying so much. The military will be good for your son."

She gave him a look of rage. "Let *me* be the judge of what is good for *my* son!" she said. But the clerk dismissed her with a wave of his hand and walked away.

Ana and Rodolfo exchanged glances.

"Let's go home, Mamá, please," he said.

"You can't stay here. I have to get you out!"

She turned around—her back now against the counter—and looked up in the distance, where the families gathered to say goodbye to their loved ones. All of a sudden, her eyes lit up, making him recall a conversation he had had with his father.

"I've never seen such dark eyes with so much light in them," his father had said about the first time he saw her. "It was as if, when she looked at you, the heavens opened and everything seemed possible."

But Rodolfo didn't have much time to think. His mother grabbed him by his hand again and pulled him towards her, as if pulling a kite. He thought she looked like a *desquiciada*—like his grandmother called her when she acted unhinged. Rodolfo's father didn't appreciate the label Ana's mother had placed on her, as if labeling a can of Russian meat. He thought Ana was often misunderstood for the same reason she shouldn't have been, because she wore her heart on her sleeve. This made her passionate and unpredictable, and above all capable of bringing the moon from the sky, if she thought this could help her family.

"Let's go," she said. "I have an idea!"

His expression turned into a frown when she started to run again.

"Really?" he asked, mortified. "Why do I have to leave? What's wrong with the military?"

"I have no time for questions," she said sternly and hurried towards one of the families.

"Excuse me," Ana said.

The young couple and their family turned around and glanced at her with an inquisitive expression, as if trying to decipher whether they knew her.

"I'm sorry to bother you, but I need your help," Ana said, looking at the young couple. "Are you by any chance traveling to Madrid?"

Chapter 1

The young woman nodded, and Ana dropped her luggage by her son and approached her, speaking at a fast pace.

"Would you mind giving up your seat to my son please? He turns sixteen tomorrow, so he *must* leave Cuba today. I have relatives in Madrid and Miami. My son will need to be in Spain for a few months before traveling to the United States. I beg you. Help my son."

The young woman exchanged glances with her husband. Then her forehead rose and her shoulders shrugged. Somehow, her husband interpreted her silence. "I'm sorry," he said, shifting his gaze to Ana. "We can't help you. We are newlyweds."

Ana gave them a look of disappointment and thanked them. Moments later, she lifted her head, scanned the families near her once again, and walked towards another one, but the response was the same. As if noticing her desperation, curious eyes turned toward Ana.

"People are staring at us, Mom," Rodolfo said. "Stop acting like a crazy woman. This is embarrassing!"

She came to a sudden stop, shrunk her eyebrows, and gave him "the look."

"Do not test me, son," she said in a low tone of voice.

He stared at her in silence, tight-lipped, but when the intensity of her gaze caused him to evade her eyes, he knew nothing he could do would deter her from her plans. Once again, she turned around and began to walk with firm, determined steps—with the assertiveness and conviction of a lioness—leaving him no option but to follow her. She approached several families at random, only to hear the same answer. No one could help her.

Time was running out.

Near the entrance of the secured pre-boarding area, Ana noticed a young couple with three small children and dashed toward them. The husband kissed his wife goodbye and embraced his daughters, both seemingly under five. Then his attention turned to the infant boy—carried in his mother's arms. He kissed the baby's forehead.

"Sir, are you traveling alone?" Ana asked him. He and his wife turned their faces toward her.

"Yes," he said as his eyebrows came together.

"Sir," she said with a worried look, her hand resting on her son's shoulder. "My son will turn sixteen tomorrow. If he doesn't leave in this flight, he'll be of military age and won't be able to leave. You're a parent like me. Please help my son."

The husband looked at his wife first, then at the children, and finally at Ana's son—who turned his eyes away in resignation.

"Please, sir," said Ana, scrunching up her face to signal her concern. "Help me save my boy."

After a moment of hesitation, he looked into his wife's eyes. She nodded. He then turned to Ana and inclined his head in agreement. Ana's eyes lit up, a wide smile transforming her expression. "Thank you!" she said, hugging him and his wife.

Later, after Ana reimbursed him for the cost of the ticket, she walked away with her son. She had only taken a few steps when she stopped and turned her face toward the man who had given up his seat.

"By the way, my name is Ana," she said with a smile. "I will never forget you."

This event would have repercussions neither Ana, her son, or the kind stranger anticipated. It was the fork in the road that would forever change their lives.

It was October 2, 1968, over nine years since the triumph of Fidel Castro's revolution.

Hundreds of people with ties to the previous government had been jailed. Those less fortunate had stood in front of Castro's firing squads, their backs against the infamous *paredón de fucilamiento*, only to have their brains scattered over the white wall behind them. The bodies, buried in mass graves, were never seen again by their families. Thousands had abandoned Cuba, including many of Rodolfo's relatives, who had left between 1959 and 1960, but his mother didn't have the money for all of the family to travel together.

Concerned by the rumors the Cuban government would take the children away from their parents to send them to work camps in the Soviet Union, between 1960 and 1962, parents—some of whom couldn't afford to leave Cuba—sent their children to the United States alone, under a program called Operation Peter Pan, created by Father Bryan O. Walsh of the Catholic Welfare Bureau. Over 14,000 children left the island without their parents during that period. But Rodolfo's mother—realizing her husband would never allow their two small children to travel alone—had decided to wait until they were older.

Six years had passed since the conclusion of Operation Peter Pan, and after many arguments with her husband and numerous sleepless nights, she had convinced him their son was old enough to travel by himself, a decision that had brought them to this time and place, to the split in her son's path which would unite his life and that of the kind stranger—whose name was Rio—in an unimaginable way.

Later, as mother and son approached the entrance to the secured area, Ana placed her hand on her son's shoulder.

"Rodolfo. Look at me, son! We have little time, and I need you to remember a few things."

She handed him his suitcase and reached for his arm while her son gave her an angry glance.

"Pay close attention to what I'm about to tell you," she said. "Eat everything they give you on the plane and drink plenty of fluids. When you arrive in Madrid, your aunt will pick you up at the airport. Please listen to her. You'll live with her for a few months, and then, when all the immigration papers are ready, you'll fly to the United States to be with your uncle."

"Fine, Mom," he responded, rolling his eyes. "I understand."

Chapter 1

"Don't worry about anything," she said. "We'll see you again soon."

He nodded, wondering for a moment whether he was angry at her for forcing him to leave or at the situation which had led her to her decision.

She gave him a kiss on the cheek. "Look at you," she said with pride in her eyes. "You're practically a man. One day, you'll understand that this was not easy for your father or me. We're doing this for you, for your future."

"You said that before, Mamá," he said looking up. "Many times." Deep down, he didn't want to act this way. He just did.

"Yes, I know! I was a teenager once, you know? I thought I had everything figured out, but then I realized how little I knew. Give me a hug, my little twig."

They embraced, he, accepting the time to let go had come, and she, urging him to break free. As she held him so close, she recalled the day of his birth; the radiance in her face when the nurse placed his tiny body in her arms; his first steps; the fear in her eyes one October night when his fever reached above forty degrees Celsius and he cried inconsolably; his itchy face covered by chicken pox; his pride when he came home with good grades; his joy when the family went to Santa Maria Beach and he and his father played catch on the sand until the sun went down. Memories she wanted to carve in her mind forever.

Chapter 1

"See you soon, little man," she said. "And remember this, I'll always love you. Go now, before you miss your flight."

He turned around, walked slowly towards the glass door, and entered the secured area without looking back.

CHAPTER 2

Feeling relieved the airplane had not fallen out of the sky, Rodolfo walked through Miami International Airport, carrying his winter coat under his arm. Much taller now than when he had left Havana, he attributed his growth spurt to all the *patatas bravas*, *paella*, and ham his aunt had fed him when he lived in Madrid. The time he spent in Spain had been much better than he'd expected, especially after he met a blond Spanish girl with deep blue eyes—a year older than him—at the start of autumn, when he and his Madrid family were spending a few days in Costa del Sol.

He had left his aunt and uncle at the hotel and walked to the beach alone. The aroma of the ocean air soothed him and evoked in him memories of Havana, although he found one key difference between the beaches he had visited in his city of birth and Costa del Sol. In the latter, majestic mountains in the distance embraced the sea. Havana was mostly flat, with the exception of the few hills he had seen when he visited the Escaleras de Jaruco, located in the eastern portion of the city, about fifteen kilometers south of Guanabo Beach. Smiling at the sight of the waves, Rodolfo ran towards the water, but after a short swim in the Mediterranean Sea, he returned to the sand, shivering and rubbing his arms. That was when he noticed the partially nude beachgoers, many of them old enough to be grandparents, and among them, a beautiful young woman.

She was sitting on the sand, wearing only a pink bikini bottom, her hair falling in curls over her breasts, and a crown of flowers adorning her head. Smiling in his direction, she ran her fingers through her hair in a playful manner and invited him to approach her by curling and straightening her index finger a couple of times. For a moment, he looked behind him, but when he realized *he* was the subject of her interest, he thought he had won the Spanish Christmas lottery. While they talked, he had a difficult time keeping his eyes off of her. Noticing his discomfort, she would occasionally burst into laughter.

They talked for a long while, her index finger making circles in the sand as she told him she had finished high school and was there vacationing with her oldest sister. She had decided to take a break before starting college.

"I'm not sure what I want to study yet. So many options," she said and sighed.

The way she spoke about her many vacations to Western European countries, South Africa, and Australia; the refined manner in which she took a sip from her mineral water; and the perfection of her manicured pink nails suggested to him she came from a wealthy family.

She inundated him with questions. *What grade are you in? Where are you from? What's your favorite food?* He told her he was starting the twelfth grade and talked about his parents in Cuba as well as his plan to travel to the United States. She seemed more interested in him when she realized he was from Cuba.

"Wow! I *love* Cuba and its people," she said with excitement, bringing her hands together as if she were going to clap. "In fact, I had a Cuban boyfriend once. You remind me of him. He was as handsome as you."

He blushed at her directness, so different from the girls he'd met before. His father had taught him to be the conqueror, and now he found himself in an awkward position, not knowing what to do.

When she seemed to have run out of things to say, she asked, "Would you like to come to my apartment for a while?"

He hesitated.

"Do you have another commitment, or are you afraid?" she asked.

"Neither," he said.

"Then, come with me."

He wasn't sure what he was getting into. His family had warned him about similar situations, which was why he kept examining his surroundings to ensure no one was watching them. Anything could have happened that night, something he realized much later, but for whatever reason, he trusted her.

Chapter 2

He picked up her bag and the colorful towel she had left on the sand while she slipped into a white, thin-cotton dress that revealed her curves. As they began to walk away from the beach toward the busy avenue, he admired the reddish sun, setting over the Mediterranean Sea. Then his eyes shifted to her, and for a moment, they locked gazes and smiled. When they crossed the avenue separating the beach from a row of hotels, she held his hand and laughed, as if noticing how cold it was. In silence, they exchanged flirtatious looks while they walked past several hotels, until they cut across the parking lot of one of them and climbed a set of stairs.

"Have you ever been with a girl before?" she asked him with a playful smile, as they approached the door to her hotel room, located on the second level of a three-story building.

He didn't answer, just looked at her.

"You make me laugh," she said. "I don't know why. You just do!"

Two hours later, as he walked back to his hotel to join his aunt and uncle, the breeze caressed his face and played with his hair. *Aida.* A name he would always remember. He took a deep breath, letting the salty air of the Mediterranean fill his lungs, while he smiled and marveled at the beauty of his surroundings: the endless row of lit hotels, the people from various countries walking on the sidewalk and speaking in their native language, the aroma of paella coming from a nearby family restaurant, the lights of the vehicles passing by.

He could have stayed with her forever.

His father would be so proud of him if he knew about his first conquest as a man. Or was it the other way around? He then thought about his mother who would not be as complimentary. She'd be angry at him for being reckless and going home with a stranger.

Two days after Rodolfo's encounter with Aida, he and his family returned home, but the memories of that trip would always make him smile.

Rodolfo found Madrid to be a fascinating city, from the famous football clubs Real Madrid and Atlético de Madrid to its historic city center. Also, his aunt and uncle had made him feel at home since the beginning by offering him not only their love, but a comfortable middle class existence, complemented by occasional visits to Plaza Mayor, the home of the Royal Palace, and weekend strolls through the Buen Retiro Park, one of the most beautiful and relaxing parks he had ever experienced. He and his family sat on the steps of its magnificent artificial lake—near splendorous statues, fountains, and monuments—to talk about Cuba.

It was there, by the lake, where he asked his aunt, "Do you miss Cuba?"

And her answer surprised him. "It is not a place we miss; it is a time and the connections we make."

Years would pass before he could understand the meaning of her words. Now, as he walked through the airport, he wondered about the life awaiting him in Miami.

Chapter 2

Rodolfo followed the other passengers to Customs and then to Baggage Claim. The more he walked through the long hallways of the airport, the more anxious he became, not only because of the loud speakers alternating between Spanish and a language he didn't understand well—which he realized was English—but because he knew little about his Miami family. He had spoken to Arturo, his Miami uncle, two weeks before he left Madrid, but Arturo was a man of few words. However, what he lacked in expressiveness, he seemed to make up in generosity. After all, it was Arturo who had paid for Rodolfo's trips and for the attorney who handled his immigration papers.

At one of the airport shops, Rodolfo noticed a store displaying a set of coffee cups with drawings of Cuba, and he thought about his home. He missed his family and hoped he would see them again soon. Above all, he missed his father Sergio, his best friend. When Rodolfo's mother had first suggested sending the children abroad, Sergio shouted at her and pounded his fists on the table. It was one of the few times Rodolfo had seen his father lose his temper. But his mother was relentless, wearing him down day by day, year after year, until Sergio had no other option but to concede.

Rodolfo had only spoken to his father once since he'd left Cuba, as international calls were costly and required a trip, by public bus, to the telephone company in Havana. After Fidel Castro assumed power, Rodolfo's parents depended on earnings from their government jobs, earnings which Ana devoted to food bought at the state-run grocery store and to purchases from the black market. While Rodolfo lived in Madrid, his mother had written to him several times, but not his father, who felt embarrassed about his poor writing skills.

After picking up his luggage from the conveyer belt and exiting Customs, Rodolfo walked to a section of the airport where people waited for arriving passengers. Rodolfo searched for his family, except he didn't know who was picking him up. While he waited, he focused on the hugs, the kisses, and the tears around him. One family in particular caught his attention. An old woman wearing a blue dress, accompanied by an old man wearing a long-sleeve *guayabera* shirt and black dress pants, approached a young family of four, her arms stretched open. The young husband and wife and their two daughters smiled at her.

"Thank you, God! Thank you for bringing me my daughter and her family," she said in Spanish, in a broken voice, her eyes full of tears looking up.

She reminded him of his grandmother, always dramatic about something, especially after his grandfather died. Like the old woman at the airport, his grandmother also radiated kindness and generosity. "You're my favorite grandchild," his grandmother would tell him, a phrase she repeated to Rodolfo's sister when his grandmother thought he wasn't listening. Still, she lived to fulfill Rodolfo's wishes. She'd managed to find the way to make him *arroz con leche* often, his favorite dish, even if she had to buy the ingredients in the illegal market at very high prices. If he had only been able to say goodbye to her, to thank her in person for her boundless love.

Little by little, the area around Rodolfo began to empty, and when almost all the passengers from his flight had left, he noticed a man who didn't seem to be in a hurry get up from his bench and slowly walk toward him. He had salt-and-pepper hair combed back neatly and wore thick glasses revealing brown eyes devoid of joy. His white polo shirt and blue pants with perfectly even creases suggested his preference for neatness and order.

"You must be Rodolfo," he said when he was about ten feet away.

Rodolfo nodded.

"I'm Arturo, your uncle. No need to call me uncle. Arturo will do. Let's go."

Arturo didn't hug him or help him with his luggage. Instead, he turned around and began to walk toward the exit of the airport with quick steps, while Rodolfo followed him, struggling to keep up.

CHAPTER 3

From the moment Rodolfo picked up the handset and said hello to his mother, all he could hear was her inconsolable sobbing. Not knowing what to do, he sat on the floral couch at his aunt's house in Madrid, waiting for his mother to regain her composure. It was the first time he had spoken to her since leaving Cuba.

"I miss you so much!" she finally said.

"I miss you too, Mami," he replied with a genuine concern in his voice. "How's everybody?"

He sounded unlike the boy who had left Cuba two weeks earlier, as if the distance had erased his immaturity. She spoke for a long time, with a rapid delivery of words, as if she were shooting them with a high-power rifle. He listened attentively, constructing the images of her story in his head.

After his airplane took off from Rancho Boyeros Airport, Ana hadn't felt like going home. She didn't want to go to an empty house or run into nosy neighbors who might have seen her earlier leaving the house with Rodolfo. She needed time to tell her family about his departure, but she realized the secret would not be kept for very long. Not in the Santos Suárez neighborhood. It was as if rumors grew giant legs and ran through every block, carrying loud speakers and announcing every intimate detail about everyone's lives. She suspected it wouldn't be long before someone in the neighborhood would tie the pieces together.

Rodolfo's twelve-year-old sister, Amanda, wouldn't return from school for another three hours, and Sergio would arrive from the furniture factory where he worked much later. Amanda didn't suspect anything. Ana didn't want to burden her with the anticipation of her brother's impending departure and believed that telling her after Rodolfo was gone would be less painful. Ana feared her mother's reaction far worst, and as she approached the three-story building on Zapote Street, where her mother Claudia and her sister shared an apartment, Ana's anticipation grew.

Claudia had not always lived with her sister. After Claudia's husband died from a massive heart attack five years earlier Claudia decided to leave her house to Ana and her family, and move in with her widowed sister. The Urban Reform Law Castro implemented in 1960, which transferred ownership of all living quarters to the government, had led to housing shortages. It made it virtually impossible for the young couple to trade the small apartment where they lived for a house.

"Mom! Aunt Alicia!" Ana yelled after allowing herself in with her own key. "I'm home."

The apartment, small and cozy, had a living room with hardly enough space to accommodate the sofa and two rocking chairs. Adjacent to it was a tiny dining room with a square wooden table and four chairs.

The walls had been painted green in 1956, when paint was still available at the stores, but the color, like Cuba, had faded. Everything was clean and orderly, and the apartment smelled like freshly-brewed coffee. An oversized picture of Fidel Castro, which angered Ana each time she saw it, hung on the dining room wall. Claudia had asked her sister to remove it, but Alicia, unlike her sister, believed in the revolution.

Ana searched in the kitchen and in the bedroom both sisters shared. The bedroom smelled like violets from her mother's favorite cologne *Agua de Violetas,* which Claudia used every time she showered. No sight of the sisters. Ana wondered if they had gone to Santos Suárez Park for a walk, as they often did, but when she returned to the living room, she noticed the thin wooden-white doors, leading to the balcony, slightly opened.

"Mom, Aunt Alicia! Are you here?" she asked. She pulled the doors open, and the screeching of the hinges gave her goosebumps.

She found Claudia and Alicia sitting comfortably on rocking chairs and watching the people go by. They wore housedresses—her mother's pink and her aunt's blue. They hardly looked like sisters. Alicia had white hair, tanned skin, and was much heavier and less wrinkled than her sister. Claudia was overly thin. She had fair skin and long white hair held back in a ponytail.

The sound of Ana's voice made them turn their heads in her direction.

"Ana, what a surprise!" said her mother, rising off her rocking chair.

"I kept calling you, but no one answered!" Ana replied, raising her eyebrows.

"You know our hearing is not what it used to be, sweetheart," said Claudia, reaching for her daughter's hand and placing it between hers.

"Ana, is everything okay?" her aunt asked, adjusting her glasses. "I thought you would be at work today."

Ana sighed. "I didn't go," she said. With a reflective look in her eyes, Ana gave each of the women a hug and a kiss on the cheek. "Something came up," she added.

Claudia glanced up at her daughter's face with an inquisitive and wondering expression. "Are the children okay?"

"Yes, Mom, they are, but we need to talk," Ana said, keeping her voice low and looking down at the streets, where an old man passed by, carrying a loaf of bread in a brown bag. "It's better if we go inside," she added.

Her mother stared at her, perplexed.

"I don't know what can be so important you can't tell me here, but sure," she said and picked up two empty coffee cups resting on a round metal table.

"You too, Aunt Alicia," Ana said when she noticed her aunt was not following Ana and her mother.

The three women went inside the apartment, and Ana, the last one to enter, closed the doors behind her.

"The two of you start without me," her aunt said. "I'll go to the kitchen and pour you a cup of coffee, Ana. I won't be long."

"Don't worry about coffee," Ana said, feeling a knot in her stomach." I'm not in the mood."

Alicia shook her head and crossed her arms. "Now, I know something is wrong," she said. "You never turn down coffee."

Ana asked the sisters to sit on the sofa, while she pulled a chair from the dining room and sat in front of them.

"You're starting to scare me, Ana," said her mother. "Did your husband hurt you? You better tell me if he did." She paused and began speaking with her hands while ranting. "Your father might be dead, but I'm here to defend you. I'll go there myself and put him in his place. Nobody hurts my daughter."

"Why are you always saying that? He loves me!" Ana replied.

Claudia waved her hand dismissively at her daughter and rolled her eyes.

"That's what you keep telling me, but I don't believe it. Your father and I *both* told you. You should've married someone of your caliber. Remember how many times we repeated it? But you refused to listen. Just like your father. May he rest in peace." Claudia made the Sign of the Cross.

"Claudia, let your daughter speak, please." Alicia said, touching her sister's hand. "Sergio loves her and the kids. I'm sure of that."

"You're always against me," said Claudia disapprovingly. "I'm your older sister, the most

26

Chapter 3

experienced of the two of us. Remember the phrase: The devil knows more from experience than from being the devil."

Alicia chuckled. "Are you saying you're the devil?"

Claudia crossed her arms and leaned back. "You're always misinterpreting everything I say!" she said. "Never mind."

Ana took a deep breath.

"Mom, Aunt Alicia. I need you to listen and stop arguing. This is very important."

"You're making me nervous," Alicia said. "Just say it. Why so much mystery?"

Ana pressed her lips before she spoke again. "You know how much I love my children. I would do anything for them."

"Of course you would," said Claudia. "You're my daughter, and I taught you well."

Alicia rolled her eyes and shook her head. "Ana, please!" Alicia said. "Stop going around in circles. What happened?"

"Well..." Ana swallowed, dry-mouthed. "You know tomorrow is Rodolfo's sixteenth birthday."

"How can I forget?" her mother said. "I was assuming you had something planned for this weekend. A cake from La Gran Vía and some punch, right?"

"There won't be a birthday party, Mom."

"Is it the money?" asked Claudia. "I know your husband doesn't make much, but I can help you."

"That's not the problem," Ana said. "Mom, Aunt Alicia... If my son had stayed here until he turned sixteen, he would not have been allowed

27

to leave. And if he had become a doctor or an engineer in Cuba, Castro could have sent him abroad who knows where. I don't want that for him. I had no choice."

"What did you do?" her aunt asked, placing her hand on her chest. "Where is he?"

"Rodolfo is on a plane to Madrid," Ana said, evading their eyes. "From there, he'll travel to the United States."

Both sisters rose off the couch. As the shock wore off, reality slipped in, and Claudia's eyes filled with emotion.

"You did what?" Claudia shouted. "How dare you! Without telling me? Why didn't you allow me to say goodbye to my only grandson? What kind of daughter does that to her mother? Do you realize what you've done to me?"

Claudia crossed her arms over her head and paced slowly around the room. Then, taking a deep breath, she gave her daughter a sad, sad look.

"Oh my God!" Claudia said, her voice cracking. "My poor grandson, out there in the world alone. What have you done?"

"I'm sorry, Ana, but your mother is right," her aunt said. "You should've spoken to her. Not telling her is unforgivable."

Ana took a couple of steps towards her mother and tried to embrace her, but Claudia stepped back, lowered her arms, and turned the palms of her hands towards her daughter, while shaking her head.

Chapter 3

"Don't touch me!" Claudia said sternly. "Don't get close to me. This is *so* wrong, Ana. You have killed me today. Please leave."

"But Mom... I knew you'd react like this. That's why I couldn't tell you. Please forgive me."

"I'm going to my bedroom," said Claudia, while her sister still seemed to be processing what she had heard. "I need a pill for my nerves. This is just too much for my heart to take."

Claudia turned around and walked away while Ana hugged her aunt goodbye and went back home.

Rodolfo had been listening to his mother's story attentively, imagining how upset his grandmother must have been.

"I've talked too much, son," Ana said. "This is going to cost a fortune. I'll write to you. Please don't forget to write back."

"Don't worry, Mamá," he replied. "I won't forget."

CHAPTER 4

A month after Rodolfo's mother called him, a letter arrived from Cuba, several pages long, hand-written on thin paper. Cecilia, his aunt in Madrid, handed it to him when he returned from school. Immediately, Rodolfo recognized her writing style, impeccable, easy to understand. He excused himself and went to his room to read it, hoping his mother would tell him something about his girlfriend.

Ana started the letter where she had left off during their first call. As he read, his ability to visualize things in his head helped him fill in the blanks.

***

After leaving her mother's house, Ana returned home, hoping for some peace and quiet, but she realized the argument with Rodolfo's grandmother was only the beginning.

She hand-washed some clothes, a task she dreaded, and hung them on a clothesline above the flat roof. Trying to stay busy, she went to Rodolfo's bedroom and began to organize his closet and his chest of drawers. She knew she had to sell what stayed behind to save money, but she didn't know if she'd be able to do it. Doing so would be like erasing him from existence.

She played with an old wood truck Rodolfo had kept from his younger years, a gift from his father. Inside one of his drawers, she also found a black-and-white picture of Rodolfo's father next to two-year-old Rodolfo and a younger version of herself. She caressed it while a tear streaked down her face as the memories of that day rushed in. It had been taken at the zoo, Rodolfo's favorite place. After a moment of quiet contemplation, she stored the picture where she had found it and went into the kitchen to finish dinner.

Ana was in the kitchen when her husband arrived, drenched in sweat. After he kissed her, she noticed a look of preoccupation contorting his expression, but instead of acknowledging it, she smiled and gave him a long hug.

"Where is Rodolfo?" he asked.

"He's gone," she said.

"What do you mean? Where?"

Realizing he knew the answer, his question bothered her.

"To Madrid, where else?" she said with an expression of incredulity. He didn't say anything. "At last, he'll have the life I wanted for him." She looked up with hopeful eyes, as if imagining the possibilities.

Shaking his head with a look of disappointment, he said: "I don't understand how you can be this happy. What if... we never see him again?"

She rubbed her forehead with her fingers. "Sergio, please! Don't think that way. You know perfectly well my brother is taking care of the papers and the money. It's only a matter of time."

He took a deep breath, and his eyes focused on a notebook his son had left on the kitchen counter.

"I can't believe he's gone," he said, grabbing the notebook and turning the pages. "If I had known you were gonna be able to buy a ticket... I would've taken off work."

Sergio read a couple of lines of his son's Spanish composition homework. "I should've been there," he said, throwing the notebook on the floor with anger. "I'm so stupid. I didn't think you would be able to pull it off, not with so many people leaving Cuba."

She picked up the notebook, placed it on the counter, and caressed his face.

"You underestimated me; that's all," she said. "But I always find a way. I talked to everyone I saw at the airport until someone agreed to give up his seat. Please don't worry. We'll see him again soon."

She spoke with conviction in her voice.

"I hope you're right," he said, unbuttoning his shirt. "You know how I feel about all this. Cuba is our home. I don't think the situation is as bad as you paint it."

"I don't want to argue about this, Sergio," she said, tucking her hair behind her ears, her eyes trying to conceal her frustration. "Each day, the government is doing more and more to take away the rights of the parents. I won't let *anyone* take our children. Kids are encouraged to report their parents to the authorities, for God's sake! Is this what you want?"

He didn't answer.

"Go shower, and I'll serve you your food," she added. "I cooked black beans and rice. The beans are exquisite."

He took off his sweaty shirt, revealing his muscular build.

"Where's Amanda?" he asked.

"Next door, at her friend's house."

"Does she know?"

"No, I wanted both of us to tell her after dinner," she said.

He gave her an empty look and walked away to avoid an argument. After all, she always claimed to know what was best for the family, making him feel inept at times, making him wonder why a smart, young woman like her, who had attended college for three years, had married someone with an eighth-grade education.

Sergio was a simple man, a carpenter whose idea of happiness was to restore old furniture six days a week. But since the day she walked into his shop with her father in 1951, wearing a black and white polka-dot dress, her flowery perfume defying the smell of wood, machines, nails, and glue, he knew all he wanted was to be with her. It was a hot July day. He was cutting a sheet of wood, his bare, muscular arms glistening with sweat. The bell on the old desk rang, and when he looked up, he noticed her staring at him.

They were married, following a short court-ship, and had two children, first Rodolfo, and four years later, Amanda, but Rodolfo was his life. Even his daughter had noticed how much her father favored her brother. He was his pride and joy.

Castro's revolution triumphed in 1959, leading to the appropriation by the new socialist government of Sergio's shop and most of his tools. His wife had warned him about the unpre-dictability of the new government and its disap-proval of private businesses. These businesses, in Castro's opinion, represented the past. The so-cialist revolution was the future. Despite his re-luctance to believe his wife with all her ide-as—injected into her head by her father, a devout capitalist—prior to the nationalization of all means of production, Sergio had taken home some of the tools and supplies, which would al-low him to keep doing private jobs to supplement the family's income.

When his son turned nine, Sergio began to teach him how to fix furniture, like his father be-fore him had taught him. The boy had a natural talent for working with wood, and Sergio could not be happier. Now, Sergio felt as if he had been torn apart.

That evening, as Ana was finishing setting up the dinner table, Amanda arrived.

"Hello, Dad!" she said and kissed him on the cheek.

He forced a smile and patted her on the back.

"Hello, pretty girl."

Chapter 4

"I don't look pretty, Dad, not with this ugly pimple on my face," said Amanda, tucking a strand of black hair behind her ear.

"You'll be a teenager soon," said Ana. "It's normal."

"A kid at school laughed at me today. I don't like people laughing at me."

"That's not a big deal, Amanda," said her mother. "Don't worry so much about small things."

"It's not nice, Mom," said the girl. "Besides, both you and Dad have taught me to defend myself, which is what I did. So I told him my big brother was gonna beat him up if he kept laughing at me." Amanda paused for a moment and looked around the room. "And where is my brother?"

Husband and wife exchanged glances.

"Don't worry about your brother," said Ana. "Let's sit down and eat dinner. It's going to get cold."

Everyone sat down, and Ana silently began to serve the food.

Amanda thanked her mother when she handed her a plate with a small serving of white rice and black beans. Amanda was pretty—like her mother—with long black hair she braided every day before she walked to school. It was too hot outside to leave her hair down, even in the month of October. She wore a pair of white shorts and a pink blouse her mother had a seamstress make for her. A girly girl, despite her father's best efforts to teach her how to work with wood, she enjoyed dancing and reading.

After Amanda swallowed the first spoonful, she said, "It's not fair, Dad. Why can my brother stay out and not me? Is it because he's a boy?"

Sergio looked down and continued to eat slowly.

"Finish your food and let us worry about what's fair," said Ana.

They remained in silence for a moment, Ana and Sergio exchanging looks as they ate.

"Did you learn a lot at school today?" Ana asked her daughter after both of them had devoured half of their food.

"Same old thing," said Amanda. "Science, Math, History... In the History class, they taught us about Lenin and Karl Marx."

Ana shook her head and stared at her husband with an *I-told-you-so* look. He avoided her eyes and kept eating.

Once everyone was done, Amanda rose from her chair.

"Sit down, please. We need to talk," said her mother.

The girl gave her an inquisitive look but obeyed.

"What did I do now? Am I in trouble?" Amanda asked.

"You're not," Ana replied. "We need to talk to you about your brother."

"Oh, so he's the one in trouble. Well, don't count on me to tell you anything. He's my brother."

"Tell us what?" Ana asked.

Amanda shrugged and sat down.

"Whatever it is that got him in trouble. You would know better than me."

Ana reached for her daughter's hand and gave it a soft squeeze.

"Amanda, I'm very proud of you. You're a good sister, and that makes me happy. But your father and I have something important to tell you."

Sergio took a deep breath and evaded his wife's gaze while Ana continued to stare at him.

"Sergio, do you want to tell her?" Ana asked.

"Me? No," he said, shaking his head. "I think you should tell her."

"Tell me what? You two are acting weird tonight."

Ana hesitated, unsure of how to respond.

"Your brother..." said Ana, and she paused for a moment. "He left this morning."

Amanda knitted her eyebrows.

"What do you mean?" she asked. "Where?"

"Madrid," Ana said.

"Spain?"

"Yes."

Amanda shot up from her chair and stared at her mother with an accusatory expression. "But why?" she asked, furrowing her eyebrows. "Why did you let my brother leave by himself? When is he coming back?"

Sergio looked away. With pleading eyes, Ana kept seeking his support, but he remained silent.

"He won't return, sweetheart," Ana said. "But don't worry. We'll see him soon. He'll be in

Madrid for a few months and then travel to the United States. A few months later, we'll join him. But please don't tell anyone, you hear me?"

"You mean, we're doing what many of my friends' families are doing? But why? Didn't Dad say that people who left Cuba were traitors to the revolution? I don't want to be a traitor. Cuba is my home."

Ana stared at her husband and then shifted her gaze to her daughter.

"Your father didn't mean it. He doesn't believe people who leave are traitors."

"But my teachers do," Amanda said with a look of defiance.

"Your teachers are wrong, sweetheart," she said.

Amanda stared at her mother with eyes filled with tears and anger. "You're the one who's wrong! You're wrong to have allowed my brother to leave by himself. I hate you!"

Amanda ran to her bedroom, the tears spilling down her face.

"I should go after her," said Ana.

"It won't help," said Sergio. "This is not easy for her or for me."

"I don't know why *everyone* keeps giving me a hard time about this decision!" Ana yelled waving her arms in the air. "This *had* to be done for our son's future."

"I hope you're right, my love," said Sergio. "I hope you're right."

***

Chapter 4

Now that Rodolfo had finished reading the long letter, he felt worse than before, unable to think of a way to make the current situation any better. He was also surprised his mother had not said anything about Susana and worried about her, thinking of her reaction when she heard he had left. He decided to write to his father and include a letter to his girlfriend inside the same envelope. But what would he tell her?

From his school backpack, he extracted an eight by eleven pad and began to write.

Hello Dad,

How are you? Are you staying busy? I'm fine, missing you all, but you taught me to be tough like you. So don't worry. I'm working hard to make you and Mom proud.

Spain is very different from Cuba. People here eat a lot. I'm not used to eating so much, but my aunt gets mad when I don't finish everything on my plate. So get ready. When you see me again, I won't look like the same skinny kid.

I know you don't like to write letters. I understand. Tell my sister to behave, okay? She doesn't have me there anymore to get her out of trouble.

Hey, I need a favor. Can you give the enclosed letter to my girlfriend? Please don't read it, and don't tell Mom.

A big hug, mi viejo. Take care of Mom and my sister. I hope it won't be much longer before your visas arrive. I'll see you soon.

Chapter 4

He signed the letter with "Your Son." Then he thought about what to tell his girlfriend. After a moment of quiet reflection, he began to write. In his letter, he told her he was in Madrid and planned to travel to the United States after a few months. He didn't know how long he would be away and made no promises to return, but he missed her.

A few months later, Rodolfo received a letter from Susana.

Dear Rodolfo:

How are you? I hope by now you've found what you were looking for when you decided to leave Cuba. I miss you. You should know I will always have a place for you in my heart, but we cannot fight our destinies. It's not fair to either one of us to ask the other to wait for a miracle. I see people leaving Cuba and saying they'll come back one day. That's what your mom told me, but... we all know that will never happen. Who would ever want to return here?

Have a great life, Rodolfo.

Susana never mentioned whether she had received his letters. His mother may have discovered them and didn't give them to her. Anything was possible. It hurt him to read her words, but they led him to conclude his ties to the life he'd left behind were unraveling at a faster pace than he'd imagined.

CHAPTER 5

As Arturo drove home from the airport without saying a word, Rodolfo felt uncomfortable. He tried to engage Arturo in conversation by thanking him for everything he was doing for his family, but he responded with a single nod. Rodolfo blamed his mother for placing him in this situation, for always getting others to act against their wishes, even if she didn't do so maliciously.

Not having anything to do, Rodolfo looked outside his window. Traffic was heavy, as in Madrid, but he noticed the architecture was very different in Miami. It lacked the vast number of impressive colonial buildings and the romanticism of a bygone era of Madrid. Miami seemed more raw and practical, with factories and shops erupting throughout the city and faces that looked like his. Judging by all the billboards in Spanish, it didn't seem to him as if he were in the United States.

The drive from the airport was only fifteen minutes, after taking the 14th Street East-West Expressway. When Arturo and Rodolfo arrived at Arturo's house, located near Calle Ocho in Miami, they found the front door open with dozens of neighbors and relatives gathered on the porch and in the living room, engaging in animated conversations. This made Rodolfo feel as if he were back in Havana. Arturo dashed past the crowd without saying a word to take refuge toward the rear of the house while Martica, his wife, greeted Rodolfo with a big familiar hug and told him, "You must be starving." And without allowing him to respond, she stuffed a ham croquette in his mouth and gave him a glass of iced Coca Cola. Around the same time, a man with a kind smile offered to take his luggage, and a woman collected his coat. While he drank the Coca Cola and greeted everyone with a shy grin, he noticed his uncle shaking his head before entering one of the rooms, but no one seemed to notice.

Martica looked like the aunt anyone would want: a smile, brilliant like a diamond, and a welcoming plump face, displaying with pride a pair of kind blue eyes hidden behind prescription glasses. Unlike many women her age, she had allowed her hair to show its natural grey. Happy like a child, she rushed to the dining room and returned with a paper plate full of food: *moros*; fried sweet plantains; two small guava pastries; and two chicken croquettes.

"Eat this," she told him.

When Rodolfo finished eating everything on his plate, he listened to the conversations going on around him. The women talked about their children and their families, illnesses, or major purchases, while the men—in an animated and loud manner—discussed politics.

Chapter 5

"There isn't a better communist than a dead one," he heard one of the men say while the three other men who surrounded him nodded in agreement.

Rodolfo approached them and listened to their stories. The brother of one of them had been shot by officials of the Castro government. The father of another man was jailed for antirevolutionary activities. A third one had been forced to work in labor camps because he wanted to leave the country. He said Castro's military men had made him dig a grave once. "This is for you," one of the guards at the camp told him. "Traitors should dig their own graves." Rodolfo noticed the consternation on the face of the man who was telling the story, his reflective eyes.

"When I was done digging, they pushed me into the ditch and pointed a gun to my head. And I'm telling you, brother, when I looked into the eyes of that guy, I was convinced that if his superior had not gotten there just in time, I wouldn't be telling you this story." His fists closed as he spoke about the past. The other men shook their heads.

Among the neighbors was a young man whose parents had sent him to the United States alone during the Peter Pan exodus. "I was ten," the young man said. "I didn't speak English and was confused when my parents put me on a plane with my favorite toy truck and a bag of clothes. On the same flight, there were a bunch of kids traveling alone, some younger than me. I later learned I was one of the lucky ones because I had relatives in Miami. But my parents are still in

Cuba." The young man looked away. Another one patted him on his arm.

Rodolfo didn't know any of these events had occurred, as his parents seldom discussed politics in front of their children. All he knew was that, as long as he could remember, his mother had wanted to leave Cuba.

After a long while, people started to leave, and his aunt led him to one of the bedrooms. His coat was on the bed, and his luggage sat near the dresser. The delicate smell of violets in the air reminded him of his grandmother's apartment in Havana.

"This is your room," Martica said, extending her arms forward. "Sorry about the pink paint. It was my daughter's bedroom, but she got married and moved away."

She paused a moment, shook her head, and sighed.

"Between you and me, it would've never occurred to me to leave my parents and move to another city," she said with melancholy. "I guess times have changed." She paused again. "You know? Clarita, my daughter, used to play a song by... I think it was Bob Dylan who sang it. It's called the *Times Are Changing*. They sure are." She shook her head. "I can't hardly recognize this country anymore. Don't get me wrong. This is still a paradise compared to what we left behind, but I get scared sometimes, when I see all these kids with Che Guevara t-shirts, who have no idea what communism is. It's so sad." She shrugged. "Anyhow, now it's just me and Arturo... But please, make yourself at home. I've talked too much. I *always* do."

"Thank you, Tía Martica," Rodolfo said, smiling at her and gave her a quick hug. "By the way, what happened to my uncle? Is he okay?"

She nodded.

"Your uncle doesn't like to be around people, but he's a good man," she said. She sat on a wooden chair across from the bed and grimaced, while she massaged her leg. "Give him time. I just served him some guava marmalade with a slice of cream cheese. That always lightens his mood."

Martica told him that although Arturo was an engineer in Cuba, he had to settle for an assistant engineer job in Miami because he didn't have the time or money to revalidate his title and his English was not strong enough. To save the money for Rodolfo's flight and legal fees, Arturo had taken a second job during the Christmas season.

According to Martica, Arturo liked the stillness of the library, the sound of pages turning, and the embrace of ink and paper. As for fiction books, what a waste of time they were, Arturo thought. History, finance, or economics books were his favorite.

Martica switched the conversation to her married daughter and her monolingual Irish husband who spoke English and a handful of words of Spanish.

"Why couldn't she have married a nice Cuban man from Miami?" she asked. "But nope! She had to do things her way. Just like her father.

Her husband's job moved him to another city, and she had to follow him."

Martica shook her head.

"These kids! But who am I to judge, right?"

Martica rose off the chair and gave Rodolfo fresh towels and soap she had stored in the dresser. She then opened the closet and reached in. In her hand, he noticed two books, one entitled "Chariots of the Gods" and an English-Spanish dictionary.

"I almost forgot," she said. "Your uncle bought these for you. He said you should not waste any time."

"What do you mean?" he asked, examining the books.

"He knows your English is not strong enough for this book, but he wants you to start reading this book and translating the words you don't know with the dictionary." She paused and shook her head. "He's very much into education. I'm sure that if you look for the words 'bookworm' in the dictionary, you'll see his face."

He laughed.

"Thank you for everything, Tía Martica," Rodolfo said with a sincere smile.

"No need to thank me," she said. "By the way, tomorrow your uncle will sign you up for school."

"But tomorrow is Friday. Can it wait until Monday?"

"Not according to your uncle. He doesn't want you to miss any classes. He says he worked too hard to give his family an opportunity to live in a free country and enjoy a good life. You have no idea how many times I've heard the *same* speech. There's no point in arguing with him. Besides, he took two days off at work. Monday he is going back to the office." Martica paused and narrowed the space between Rodolfo and her before proceeding. "Between you and me," she whispered, looking occasionally towards the entrance of the room, "I think his strictness is one of the reasons our daughter moved so far away. I don't believe it was because of her husband's job."

"Where does she live?" he asked.

"New York City. She's a nurse, but your uncle wanted her to be an engineer, like he was in Cuba. They fought so much about it."

"What's wrong with being nurse?"

"Nothing. He said that if she wanted to go into healthcare, she should've been a doctor. He thought she was taking shortcuts." Martica paused for a moment and straightened an issue of *T.V. Guide* sitting on top of the dresser. "Oh, one more thing, no Spanish television."

He looked at her with a furrowed brow.

"What do you mean?" he asked.

"You can only watch the English-language channels. This little booklet can tell you what programs are available."

"But Tía Martica, my English is not very good."

"That's the point. Your uncle told me the more you expose your ears to the language, the easier you will pick it up," she said, raising her hands, her palms facing him. "These are his rules, not mine. Like the Americans say, don't kill the messenger." Her eyes widened and her eyebrows rose as she tilted her head. "But he does have a point, you know? I have been married to that man for many years. I know he means well."

She remained wrapped in thought for a moment while her eyes focused on a picture on top of the dresser. She picked it up and gave it to Rodolfo.

"This is your cousin Clarita with your uncle and me. She was sixteen in that picture. Your uncle had taken us to Disney World in Orlando, but he was too thrifty to stay at a hotel, so we drove back to Miami that evening. He swore not to ever go there again."

"Why not?"

"He said it was a waste of money. If she wanted to have fun, she should go to museums. He doesn't understand you can't force a child to become what that child doesn't want to become."

She took a deep breath. "Enough about your uncle. Let me get back and clean up the mess."

"Where is my uncle?"

"Reading; that's what he likes to do."

"I'll help you with the cleaning," said Rodolfo.

"That's a woman's job. You concentrate on your reading."

"My father helps my mother with the dishes," said Rodolfo.

"Really?" his aunt said, raising her eyebrows. "You're going to make a woman very happy one day. Not only are you handsome, but you are also useful around the house. I already like you!"

He smiled and, despite her insistence she could handle the cleaning, he followed her to the kitchen and began to wash dirty dishes.

In the evening, when the house came alive with the news broadcasts, Rodolfo watched footage of protestors all over the country. The Vietnam War was the culprit for the uproar. Messy and complicated. No winners, like all wars. He noticed his uncle moving uncomfortably in his seat, but Arturo restrained the urge to speak. Maybe because it was Rodolfo's first night at his house.

The next day, Arturo enrolled Rodolfo at Miami High School where he would start the twelfth grade. It was big school, bigger than the ones in Cuba. In Miami, the kids wore no uniforms, and some dressed nicer than others. Those kids who had many friends appeared happier than others. Then, there were the loners. Rodolfo wondered which type he would become.

On the first day, during the algebra class, as Rodolfo looked around the room, frazzled, struggling to decipher what the teacher was saying, a geeky young woman, with long black hair and hazel eyes hidden behind brown plastic-frame glasses whispered to him in Spanish: "Do you need help?"

The male teacher stopped his lecture and looked in their direction. "Could you please wait until the end of my class to engage in conversation?"

"I was only trying—" she said.

"Do not interrupt my class again, young lady," the teacher said.

When the teacher turned around again to write on the blackboard, she wrote something on a piece of paper and handed it to him. He glanced at it for a brief moment. "I will explain it later," the note said in Spanish.

Later at lunch, when Rodolfo was eating pizza in the cafeteria, Lissy came over with her tray and sat next to him. He greeted her with a warm smile.

"Sorry I got you in trouble with the teacher," he told her in Spanish.

"It wasn't your fault," she said. "It was mine. I should've known better than to disrupt Mr. Grumpy's class."

They both laughed.

"That's how you call him?" he asked.

"Yes," she said. "He's awful."

"By the way, my name is Rodolfo. And you?"

"Lissy," she said, tucking her hair behind her ear. "Short for Lissette."

"Isn't that a French name?" he asked.

"Yes, but I'm not French. My parents and I were born in Cuba."

"Me too!" he said.

"When did you and your parents leave?"

"My mother and I left in 1961, but my father was in jail then, so he stayed behind."

He looked at her with a puzzled expression. "In jail? Why?"

She became reflective and took a sip of her chocolate milk. "I'd rather not talk about it," she replied. "Why focus on sad things? My mother always says life is too short to spend it worrying about things we can't control."

"She has a point," he observed. "So where do you and your mom live?"

"In Little Havana, like people call that area," she said, taking another sip of milk. "Near Calle Ocho."

"Me too!" he said.

"I live with my mom and my stepfather," said Lissy with a little shrug of her shoulders.

"Stepfather? What about your dad? Did he get out of jail?"

"I told you. I don't want to talk about it." Suddenly, Lissy looked serious and sad.

"Sorry, I didn't mean to upset you," he said.

"Don't worry," she said, playing with her fingers. After a short silence, she straightened her posture and glanced at him with a forced smile. "So... who do you live with?"

"My aunt and uncle. My parents are still in Cuba."

"Sorry about that," she said with a concerned look in her eyes. "Why?"

"I'd rather not talk about it," he said, raising his eyebrows. She stared at him with pressed lips.

"Fine," she said with an assertive nod. "I respect your privacy."

He gave her a playful smirk. "Let's do this. I will share my story with you when you share yours with me."

Adjusting her glasses, she gave him an exasperated look. "Fine, just don't hold your breath."

She reached into her backpack, extracted a piece of paper, wrote something on it, and handed it to him.

"My address and telephone number," she said with authority. "I can help you with homework and anything else you need."

"Why are you being so nice to me?" he asked.

She shrugged her shoulders then relaxed them.

"I know what it's like to be in a new place and not understand the language. When we first arrived, I wished I could've had someone to help me. Besides, you seem nice."

"Thank you," Rodolfo said with a big smile. "You too."

He looked at her for a moment with a curious gaze, ignoring the students who walked by. Then, all of a sudden, she gathered her belongings and rose off her chair.

"I have to go now," she said without looking at him.

"But you haven't finished your lunch."

"I have some homework to finish before my next class. Call me tonight, okay?"

She turned around and barreled out of the cafeteria without picking up her tray. Rodolfo watched her petite figure, her heavy backpack on one shoulder, and her clumsy movements. She was wearing blue jeans, white sandals, and a pink sleeveless blouse, exposing her thin arms.

Chapter 5

Despite the heavy load, she walked fast with short strides and disappeared in the crowd of kids coming in and out of the cafeteria. He stared at her plastic tray, half full, the bread still intact. He grabbed the white roll and devoured it, ignoring the tiny pack of butter near the edge of her tray, wondering what had caused her sudden reaction.

CHAPTER 6

Arturo was sitting on the sofa reading the newspaper when Rodolfo approached him slowly, making loud footstep sounds to get his attention. Arturo continued reading without acknowledging his presence, drinking, in small sips, the large cup of *café con leche* Martica had set on the end table earlier.

"I'm meeting a friend this morning to work on my homework," Rodolfo said.

Arturo glanced at him from above his glasses. "Good," he said. He then immersed himself in his reading without saying another word, leaving Rodolfo standing in front of him.

"I finished the book you gave me," Rodolfo added.

"Remind me to lend you one of my engineering books later," Arturo replied without lifting his eyes from the pages.

Rodolfo remained motionless, waiting for his uncle to say something else, but after a long and uncomfortable while, he gave up.

"See you later, Uncle."

"I told you not to call me Uncle," Arturo said without looking at him.

Rodolfo glanced at him, trying to figure out how he could get more than a few words out of him and why he treated him like this. Since his arrival, Rodolfo had done everything he could to win him over. He mowed the lawn, took out the garbage, fixed things around the house, but nothing he did seemed to be enough. Not even a thank you from his uncle.

"Sorry, Arturo; it won't happen again," Rodolfo replied. He then turned around, picked up his backpack from the rocking chair, and left the house.

It was Saturday, two weeks after Lissy and Rodolfo met in class. Since then, other than at school, the teens had only spoken over the telephone. On this particular day, Lissy had invited him to her house.

As Rodolfo walked by the cafes lining that section of Calle Ocho, he thought about Lissy. He was thankful to have met her. Most teens stayed away from those who spoke little or no English, and he didn't enjoy feeling like an outsider. Lissy not only made him feel at home, but she was different from any other girl he had met. He could talk to her for hours and, for the most part, be himself around her. Yet, there were things about himself he didn't want to reveal to her, or to anyone, for fear of being considered weak, or not manly enough. His father had taught him men did not show their emotions to anyone and should face issues head-on. And he tried, but his fears and insecurities kept getting in the way. He wondered if other teenagers felt like him. At school, some of them acted like they had everything figured out, especially the boys on the foot-ball team. He asked himself whether everyone faced the same fears. Had some learned to create a persona to conceal how they felt?

When he arrived at Lissy's house, she came to the door with a playful smile on her face. She wore a pair of blue jeans and a white blouse, and held her hair up in a ponytail. She wore pink lip-stick and eyeliner, a departure of no-make-up look she brought to school.

"I like your cologne!" Lissy said after she greeted him with a kiss on his cheek.

He laughed. "My aunt sprayed me with my uncle's Pierre Cardin cologne before I left the house. Sorry, I must smell like a perfume store... By the way, you look pretty."

A slight flush colored her cheeks. "Thank you for the compliment, and no, you don't smell like a perfume store. It's very pleasant." Then turning her head slightly to face the rear of the house, she announced nervously: "Mom, Jerry, Rodolfo is here!"

Lissy and Rodolfo spoke in Spanish for a while, alternating between jokes about their grumpy teacher and details about the latest epi-sodes of *Hawaii Five-0*, one of Lissy's favorite shows. Rodolfo preferred to watch *Doctor Who*, *The Jetsons*, and *Star Trek*. Randomly, Lissy kept looking toward the rear of the house, growing im-patient and nervous, forgetting she had not asked him to come in or sit down. He was still standing on the porch by the front door.

After a few minutes, her hands came to-gether in a single clap, followed by: "Let me go get

Mom and my stepfather. They're in the back... I'm sorry, I forgot. Please come in and sit down!"

The conversation had come to an abrupt end, leaving him mid-sentence and confused. He sat on the brown leather sofa, wondering what had triggered her reaction. Unable to find a logical explanation, he shrugged his shoulders and began to examine the pictures on the wall. One, of a young couple with a little girl caught his attention. The man had thick, black hair and a thin mustache, and the woman, long brown hair reaching down to her shoulders. Both adults held the black-haired girl by the hand while the toddler smiled and looked up at who he assumed was the father.

He concluded the girl in the picture had to be Lissy.

"Mom, Jerry," said Lissy, in Spanish, when she returned with her mother and her stepfather. "This is Rodolfo."

Jerry O'Donnell, tall, with reddish hair and blue eyes, welcomed him in Spanish with a firm handshake, while Sara, Lissy's mom—a woman in her forties with long black hair and creamy white skin like her daughter—hugged him.

"I have heard so much about you!" she said. "I can see why."

Lissy opened her eyes wide at her mother who, with the movement of her lips, said "I'm sorry." Sara then turned to Rodolfo.

"Before you start working on your homework, I wanted to let you know we'll be taking you to lunch," Sara said. "Jerry had suggested Versailles, a popular Cuban restaurant, but have you eaten burgers before Rodolfo?"

Rodolfo shook his head.

"No, but don't worry," Rodolfo said. "I had a big breakfast, and my aunt is cooking lunch."

"It's no bother at all," Sara said, waving her hand. "Just call your aunt and tell her you will be joining us. We could take you to McDonald's instead and introduce you to hamburgers, fries, and apple pies. You'll love them!"

Opening his eyes wide and shrugging his shoulders, Rodolfo glanced at Lissy. She smiled, acting less nervous than before.

"It'll be fun!" Lissy said with glistening eyes. "I love apple pies!"

Rodolfo shrugged again. "Fine. I'll call my aunt," he said.

Sara pointed at the telephone on one of the end tables.

"Well," said Jerry after Rodolfo called his aunt, "the two of you can study here in the living room. We'll leave you alone. I suppose I can trust you with our daughter."

"I'm not your daughter, Jerry," said Lissy.

"Sorry, I meant to say my step-daughter," replied Jerry.

"Lissy, Jerry has been more than a father to you," said Sara, crossing her arms.

"It's okay," said Jerry. "Let's leave them alone so they can study. We'll see you later."

Jerry walked towards the rear of the house, while Sara stared at her daughter with an angry look.

"We'll talk later, Lissy. You had no right to treat Jerry this way."

Lissy looked down and didn't say anything. After a few seconds of a silent stare, her mother turned around and followed her husband.

"Am I missing something?" Rodolfo asked when he and Lissy were alone again.

Her face showed a mixture of anger and regret. "I don't want to talk about it."

"Is your dad in Cuba?" asked Rodolfo.

Lissy's eyes filled with tears. "Please stop asking questions," she said. "Let me bring my books."

He didn't understand what had made her so upset, but he decided to focus on the homework assignment. They studied for a couple of hours: trigonometry, chemistry, and English. She read each homework assignment to him, while he eyed the words. Then, she translated the assignments and asked him to read the instructions back to her in English. He already knew some of the words from the English classes he had attended in Spain, but his vocabulary was limited.

Around noon, Jerry and Sara reappeared.

"Time for lunch!" said Sara.

"Rodolfo, this will be a good introduction to America," said Jerry with joy in Spanish, as if he had forgotten Lissy's spitefulness. "Nothing better than a burger and an apple pie."

"Thank you for the invitation," said Rodolfo. "When I get a job, I'll return the favor."

Jerry smiled with a dismissive wave of his hand before he headed for the door, followed by his family and Rodolfo. An impeccable white Cadillac Deville with leather interior awaited outside under the carport. Jerry sat at the driver's seat, his wife next to him, while Lissy and Rodolfo slid into the back seat.

As Jerry drove, Rodolfo admired the interior of the car and compared it in his mind to his uncle's old Chevrolet. The odometer in the Cadillac read 5,126 miles compared to 106,000 miles in the Chevrolet. He imagined what his uncle would say about such a marvelous display of mechanical ingenuity: "Wasteful and pretentious!" Those would be his exact words. He would go on to say that in Cuba people kept an old car for years, and there was no reason to purchase a new car.

"Rodolfo, do you like this car?" asked Jerry, looking at him from the rear-view mirror as if he had noticed Rodolfo's expression.

"Yes, very much!" Rodolfo replied.

Jerry smiled with pride. "It has a 472 V-8 engine. If I didn't have the family in the car, I could show you its power."

Sara rolled her eyes. "Boys and their cars," she said.

"That's right," replied Jerry. "And there's nothing wrong with that."

Sara shook her head, and they all remained in silence for a moment.

"Have you chosen a career yet, Rodolfo?" asked Sara.

"My uncle thinks I should become an electrical engineer," he said.

"Good choice," said Jerry.

"Lissy wants to be a doctor, like her father," Sara said.

"I didn't know you were a doctor, sir," Rodolfo said.

"I'm talking about Sara's birth father," Sara replied. "He died in Cuba."

Rodolfo gave Lissy a caring look.

"Sorry for your loss," said Rodolfo. "I didn't know."

With her eyebrows pulled down together, Lissy looked in the direction of her mother. "Can we stop talking about my father, Mom?"

Rodolfo tried to get Lissy's attention, but she evaded his eyes and instead, lips pressed, she stared at one side of her mother's face.

"Lissy's right, Sara," said Jerry. "Let's talk about food. I'm having two cheeseburgers, fries, and an apple pie."

Sara turned her head towards her husband and crossed her arms.

"Do you have a death wish?" she asked. "All that food will clog your veins. The doctor already told you to watch what you eat."

"I'm as strong as a bull," he replied. "Don't worry. There are a lot of miles on this Irish man's odometer."

Lissy said little during the rest of the trip, her pensive eyes watching the city go by. Having listened to the exchange between Lissy and her mother, Rodolfo felt confused. Why didn't she tell him? As much as he wanted to know what had happened to her father, he decided not to bring up the topic again.

Chapter 6

When they arrived at McDonald's, Rodolfo ordered a hamburger, but Jerry added fries and an apple pie to his order and requested the same meal for himself. Sara and Lissy skipped the fries and burgers and opted for a fish sandwich and apple pie.

While they ate, Rodolfo complimented Jerry on his Spanish. Jerry explained he was born in New Jersey. His parents died when he was a baby, and a Cuban family adopted him, which allowed him to grow up speaking English and Spanish.

"Do you have a girlfriend, Rodolfo?" Sara asked after they had finished their lunch.

Lissy's cheeks turned pink.

"No, not a lot of time for girlfriends between school and work. I did have a girlfriend in Cuba."

His statement caused Lissy to look in his direction.

"Are you still communicating with her?" Sara asked.

"I wrote to her a couple of times, but after a while, we both realized it wasn't going to work."

"You heard that, Lissy?" Sara said, raising her eyebrows.

"Mom, please stop doing what I think you're doing. Rodolfo and I are just friends."

Lissy glanced at Rodolfo for a quick moment, as if trying to measure his reaction. He looked at her, smiled, and shook his head.

CHAPTER 7

When Rodolfo accepted Lissy's invitation to her cousin Lily's wedding, the last thing he suspected was Arturo's reaction. By then, Rodolfo had already secured a job at a Sedano's grocery store and worked sixteen to twenty hours a week. He announced the news to Arturo and Martica during dinner.

"That's wonderful!" Martica said. "You need a distraction. All you do is work and study." She paused for a moment and looked up with a happy expression. Then, she brought her hands together below her chin. "Besides, I like Lissy. I can't wait to see the two of you—"

But she couldn't finish her phrase. It had taken Arturo a little longer to process what his nephew had said and, as he did, he sprang into action.

"A wedding at the Fontainebleau Hotel?" His uncle blared out, speaking with his hands, an inquisitive look in his eyes. "You'll need a proper suit for that. Do you know how expensive suits are?"

"A suit?" Rodolfo asked, thinking about a wedding he had attended in Cuba two years before left. He didn't remember any of the guests wearing suits.

"Arturo, don't be that way," said Martica. "Let the boy have some fun."

"Fun?" Arturo asked. "What about his responsibilities? Do you think his family in Cuba is having fun?"

"It's not a big deal," Rodolfo replied. "I don't have to go. Your house. Your rules."

"Well said," Arturo replied with an affirmative movement of his head. "So this is the end of this discussion."

"Arturo, we don't have to be so tough with the boy," Martica said. "You see all those young people out there with long hair who don't work and are always protesting against the government. If he were like them, I would understand. But Rodolfo is a good boy. I'll go to a thrift shop and see what I can find. He already has dress pants. All he needs is a sports jacket."

"I already said no," Arturo said.

"Look," Martica pleaded. "I'll pay for it myself. I have a few alterations to make for our neighbors next door."

"Don't worry, Tía Martica," said Rodolfo. "The two of you already do more than enough for me and my family."

Martica stared at her husband with a serious expression while he kept eating, evading her eyes. When she failed to get his attention, she crossed her arms and gave him an angry look, which he also ignored.

"Martica, did you buy more Café Bustelo?" Arturo asked after having consumed most of his food. "Some guava marmalade with cream cheese would be nice too."

She didn't answer.

"Martica, my love, I'd love a cup of coffee and some dessert," Arturo said, glancing at his wife.

Still no answer from Martica, her eyes avoiding his and a serious expression on her face. Rodolfo looked at the two of them, not knowing what to do. After a long silence, Arturo took a deep breath.

"Fine, Martica," Arturo said. "I don't want to argue about this. Let me know how much the jacket is... at that store you were talking about."

Martica did everything possible to conceal her joy.

"Yes, I can make you a cup of coffee after I finish eating my dinner," she said and continued eating.

That night, Martica took her nephew's measurements, and the next day she made it her mission to find him a sports jacket to complement his beige dress pants. Later that week, when Rodolfo returned from work, his aunt greeted him with a big smile.

"It's on your bed," she said. "Try it on, and let me know what you think."

"What's on my bed?" Rodolfo asked.

"What do you think?" she asked. "Your jacket!"

Rodolfo smiled and gave his aunt a hug.

"Tía Martica," he said. "I appreciate what you've done, but I don't want my uncle to get mad at me and kick me out of this house."

"Never mind him," she said. "He's never going to kick you out of this house. Come on. Go try it on!" She smiled and followed him to his room.

Rodolfo swung the garment over his head and slid his arms into it one at a time. As he waited for his aunt's reaction, he noticed her eyes full of tears.

"Oh my God!" she said. "You look *so* handsome." And before she could help herself, drops of happiness rolled down her face.

"Why are you crying?" asked Rodolfo.

Martica's emotions kept pouring out of her as she glanced at her nephew with the tenderness and pride of a mother.

"Must be my hormones," she said, wiping her face.

Rodolfo looked at himself in the mirror.

"It looks good," he said. "But please, tell me how much I owe you."

"It's nothing," she said. "It's my gift to you."

"Why would you do that?" he asked. "You already do so much."

"It's nothing," she said. "It's just that in the few months you've lived in this house, you have earned my love. You're a good young man, not to mention a great handyman. I can't believe what you've done with our living room tables. They look brand new! Your father taught you well."

She caressed his face.

"I wish I had a boy like you," she added. "But, what am I saying? You already have a mom and a dad who love you."

"Tía Martica, you've been like a mother to me," he said. "Even when my parents arrive, nothing will change. Come on. Let me give you a hug, and stop crying."

They embraced.

"You're very sweet," she said. "I can't wait to see the two of you dressed up for the party. By the way, how are you getting there?"

"Her parents are picking me up," he said.

"As it should be," said Martica. "The more I hear about that girl, the more I like her."

Rodolfo smiled and looked at Martica with pensive eyes.

***

As Rodolfo stood in front of the mirror combing his hair, Martica walked in and, without warning, sprayed either side of his neck with Pierre Cardin cologne.

"Now you're ready!" she said, her eyes gleaming with pride. "But let me look at you. Come on, turn around."

He complied, and as he did, Martica's eyes opened wide. The blue blazer, complemented by a white long-sleeve shirt and a blue stripped tie he had borrowed from Arturo, looked perfect on him. Martica glanced at him in awe.

"You look so much like—" she said, but she didn't finish her phrase.

"Who?" he asked.

"Ah... don't mind me. I'm just imagining things. You look very handsome. That's all."

The sound of the bell interrupted their conversation.

"Oh my God!" Martica said, clapping her hands a couple of times, like a child who had won a prize. "They're here. I can't wait to see the two of you together."

The slap of her flip flops echoed as she dashed towards the living room, followed by Rodolfo. When she opened the door and Lissy appeared behind Jerry and Sara, Martica's mouth opened in astonishment.

"You look like a princess," Martica said as Lissy entered her living room, looking like royalty. Her hair, in a classic half-up style, cascaded over her back. She wore a long, rose-colored dress with off-the shoulders of beaded lace that accentuated her body. For the first time, she was wearing contacts, allowing her eyes, etched by a thin line of brown eye pencil, to glisten.

"You look beautiful," Rodolfo said, glancing at her with an interest she had not arisen in him before.

"Thank you," she said with a graceful smile.

Martica invited them in and offered them coffee.

"We're running late," said Jerry, who in his white tuxedo looked like a television celebrity. Sara's elegant dark blue dress, long and strapless, and a shimmering silver shawl, complemented her husband's attire. "Please say hello to Arturo," added Jerry.

"Of course," she said. "You must excuse him. He wasn't feeling well tonight and went to bed early." Trying to remain inconspicuous, she looked towards the rear of the house. "Well... you enjoy yourselves and take lots of pictures!"

Moments later, she watched from her porch as the two couples entered Jerry's car.

***

The wedding ceremony was taking place at the Plymouth Congregational Church, located on Devon Road in the Coconut Grove neighbor-hood of Miami.

"You want to hear something funny?" Jerry asked as he drove to the wedding ceremony. "Some people call this church the Devil's Church." He waited for a reaction, and when he noticed the smirk on Sara's face, he added, "I'm not kidding!"

He shared stories from his younger years, when he would drive his friends to the solitary dark building—in the middle of the night—to spook them by telling them exaggerated tales of what had occurred there. People said that a hooded, freaky man could be seen sometimes, roaming around the buildings of the church and scaring people away.

From the back seat, Lissy and Rodolfo listened to Jerry and smiled.

"Jerry, no more 'Devil's Church' talk after we arrive at the ceremony," Sara reminded him, glancing at him with a playful smile, her arms crossed.

"Why not?" he asked, looking at her for a brief moment and then focusing on the traffic.

Sara shook her head. "What am I gonna do with you?" she asked.

Rodolfo found the architecture of the church impressive. Modeled after a Mexican mission, it had stone walls, adorned by green vines, which made him feel as if he had traveled into a different time and place.

For the most part, Jerry behaved himself throughout the ceremony, except for the couple of times he whispered "devil's church" in Ana's ear, while she elbowed him, trying to keep her composure. On several occasions, as Lissy and Rodolfo listened to the priest, they exchanged glances and smiles. Rodolfo also looked around the room, noticing that the males were wearing tuxedos or suits. Feeling underdressed for the occasion, he looked at his beige pants and blue blazer and straightened his tie. He then examined his unpolished shoes, which had seen better days, and for the first time, he found himself to be unworthy of Lissy's company. He thought he had done her a disservice by accepting her invitation.

When the ceremony ended, and the bride and broom exited the church, cousins and friends greeted Lissy, complimenting her on her dress and her hair. Few cared to know the identity of the young man by her side, although Lissy was quick to introduce Rodolfo. Everyone spoke to her in perfect English, with occasional words of Spanish thrown in, almost as a reminder that a Cuban still lived within them but perhaps not for long.

Following the event at the church, a caravan of cars drove to the Fontainebleau Hotel for the reception. As Jerry's car approached the hotel, its modern architecture and unique construction style fascinated Rodolfo. But even more extraordinary were the lobby of the hotel and the ballroom where the reception was held.

That night, as Rodolfo danced with Lissy under hundreds of tiny lights that looked like stars, they found themselves swallowed by clusters of couples dancing around them. He wanted to tell her so much but said nothing. He could see her eyes, shining with admiration for him, seeing in him what no one else could, not even himself.

For one night, she had become Cinderella for him. That evening, her eyes unveiled the quiet magnificence of the girl—who sat by him at the school cafeteria—hiding behind her geeky eyeglasses, while eating a hotdog with only mustard.

CHAPTER 8

While Rodolfo familiarized himself with life in the United States, events were unfolding in Cuba that would forever change his parents' lives, his, and those of many of his countrymen with ties to the exterior.

**

The news in the Havana neighborhood spread like a forest fire. Everyone, even the mailman, when he walked from house to house delivering the mail, was talking about it. Rodolfo's grandmother rushed to her daughter's house as soon as she heard it. She was angry, but at the same time anxious to tell Ana *Te lo adverti, mija.* She had warned her daughter many times when Rodolfo and his sister were younger and parents were sending the children out of Cuba alone. Children had no business traveling to a foreign country without their parents. That's what she said. The latest news, she thought, had proven her right.

Chapter 8

Each neighbor had their own opinion about the proclamation made by the government, but those who opposed the decision, afraid of the repercussions, kept it to themselves and only spoke to close relatives about it.

Claudia encountered several neighbors along the way who wanted her opinion about the new measure. She had none. The government did what the government felt it was best. Who was she to judge? That was what she said, but deep down, her anger grew with each passing hour.

She felt breathless when she climbed the few steps leading to the front porch of one of the colonial-style houses on Zapote Street. Noticing then she had left the house in a *bata de casa* without a bra and with curlers covering half of her head, she thought about her husband. Never would she have left the house looking like that when he was alive. But at this moment, bigger issues occupied her thoughts. She knocked on the door.

"Ana, my love! It's me," she said.

When after a few seconds she heard no response, she used her key to allow herself in.

"Ana!" she shouted from the living room. "Are you home?" She must be at work, she told herself. Claudia was about to turn around when, from the rear of the house, she heard a faint cry. "Ana, is that you?

"Yes!" a voice replied.

Claudia rushed to Ana's bedroom, but by the time she found her, Claudia realized she already knew. Only *that* would explain her condition.

"Mamá! What have I done? How long will it be before I see my son again?"

Claudia wanted to reproach her, but when she saw her in bed with red eyes and her face wet with tears, she said none of the things she'd planned to say.

"Let me bring you some water," Claudia said, patting her daughter's arm. "You need to calm down."

She'd thought about making her one of her *cafecitos*, which in her opinion cured everything —even grief—but she remembered the words from one of Ana's doctors, from the last time Claudia accompanied her daughter to the hospital. The night before the urgent hospital visit, the electricity had gone out, and a piece of veal, Ana had stored in the fridge, went bad. After spending an extraordinary amount of money on the veal in a black market purchase, Ana didn't want it to go to waste, so she seasoned it, cooked it, and ate it. No one else in her family had touched the steak, but Ana had to prove to everyone it was safe to eat. The rest was history. During the visit to the hospital, the doctor told Ana she was hypertensive and advised her to cut down on her coffee consumption.

Claudia left the room and returned with a tall glass of water and ice.

"Come on. Sit down and drink some."

Her daughter straightened herself in the bed and reached for the glass.

"How can the government do this, Mamá?" she asked, glancing at her mother with her eyes full of tears. "How can they force people to stay?"

"There has to be a solution, my love. Come on. Take a sip of water."

Ana drank about half a glass. Then Claudia set it down on top of the night stand and caressed her daughter's hair.

It was May 31, 1970. In an attempt to mitigate the professional drain, resulting from the massive exodus out of Cuba, the Castro government had abruptly decided to prohibit the emigration of its citizens. Overnight, thousands of families found themselves separated by an invisible iron gate.

"I have to do something!" Ana said, flickering her hair behind her ears. "They can't do this to us."

"But what can you do?" Claudia said, speaking with her hands.

"I need to go to the immigration office. They have to let us leave."

"But you don't even have your visas."

"Arturo told me everything would be ready by next week. They have to make an exception."

Claudia opened her arms, and mother and daughter embraced.

"I hope you're right, my child," said Claudia, caressing her daughter's hair.

Claudia had been more forgiving than Sergio. For the next three nights, Ana slept in her bedroom alone because after Sergio heard the news, he couldn't look at his wife without exploding into an angry rant. On the fourth night, after lying on the sofa for a while, unable to fall asleep, he took a bus to the telephone company to call his son. When he arrived, he found a line of anxious people wrapped around the building, waiting for their turn to place a call. By the time his turn arrived, it took a long while for his call to connect, and by the time it did, no one picked up. He returned home frustrated and found his wife in the living room with a glass of rum in her hand.

"I can't continue to live like this," she said looking at him with an expression of defeat. "Can we talk?"

"There's nothing to talk about," he said.

"The visas and the money arrived today," she replied, looking down. Then she finished her drink. He could smell the alcohol on her breath from where he stood. "But don't worry," she proceeded, with a calm, empty voice. "You know me. There's nothing I can't do. I'll find a way. *That*, I promise you."

He looked at her with a serious expression, while Ana's eyes remained fixed on the empty glass. She looked so broken to him, it was difficult to continue to ignore it. That night, he slept in his bed, but he didn't show her any affection. Ana hardly slept, listening to his breathing, longing for his touch and for evidence she had not lost him too. He lay awake for a while, and when she touched his hand with her fingers, he pushed her hand away.

After he fell asleep, she turned towards him and watched him, wishing she could see him happy again—the way he was before their son left. If he only knew how much she loved him, a love that had grown through the years with every small detail, from the jasmines he brought her stolen from a stranger's garden to the glow in his eyes when his children were born.

She thought about her father. When he was approaching the moment of his death, he made her promise him she would not allow his grandson to become a man in Cuba or be sent to war in the name of communism. He had noticed the country's growing alliance with China and the Soviet Union, the communist slogans, the disappearance of freedom. She made him a promise and fulfilled it. Now, she promised herself to do everything in her power to reunite the family again, but not in Cuba.

The next morning, she told her husband she would take time from work to go to the immigration.

"Don't worry," she said. "I'll take care of everything. I need you to believe me."

He looked at her with hopeful eyes and kissed her on the cheek before he left. After drinking a cup of *café con leche* and eating a piece of hard bread topped with vegetable oil and salt, she showered and wore her nicest dress, rose color with a flowing skirt, a pearl necklace her father had given her when she turned eighteen, and a pair of beige heels. She let her hair down, sprayed on a perfume her sister had sent her from Spain, and took a cab to the immigration building from the nearby *piquera*. On her way, while she observed the city passing by, the families taking their children to school or non-school-age children playing with their loved ones in the park, she kept telling herself she could not give up.

Chapter 8

Interrupting her thoughts, the cab driver asked her why she was going to immigration.

"It's about my son," she answered and looked down.

The driver watched her through the rearview mirror, waiting to hear more, but when she offered no additional details, he didn't insist.

Upon arrival to the immigration building, Ana stood at the end of the long line of people awaiting their turn. After a while, an officer—tall, fit, with pepper color hair—ignoring everyone else in front of her, approached her and asked her to follow him.

People whispered as she abandoned her place in the line and followed the officer through a long corridor. At the end, there was a white door. He opened it, closed it after she entered the room, and invited her to sit down.

He sat behind his desk, leaned back on his chair, and interlaced his fingers.

"What's the purpose of your visit?" he asked.

She explained her case, and as she did, he began to play with his pen. After she finished, he said:

"I think I can help you."

"How?"

"I'm a well-connected man with a great deal of influence." He paused for a moment and looked at her, as if trying to anticipate her reaction to what he was about to say. "Why don't we discuss this over dinner?" he added.

"Over dinner?" she asked.

"Yes, at my apartment."

Chapter 8

"Could we meet at a different place?" she asked.

He remained silent for a moment.

"Look. As you can imagine, I cannot help everyone, and I don't think it's appropriate for me to meet someone who's leaving the country in public. This is a very delicate matter," he said.

"So, the only way you can help me is if we meet in your apartment?"

"Yes."

The intensity of his gaze made her uncomfortable. Then she thought about her son. How would he react when he learned he would not be able to see his family for who knew how long? She also thought about her husband and the hope in his eyes before he left the house earlier that morning.

"So if I go to your apartment… you *can* get my family out of Cuba?" she asked.

He nodded.

"I will do everything I can after we discuss your case in greater detail," he responded with conviction. He proceeded to scribble something on a piece of paper and handed it to her.

"Come to this address after 6 p.m. tonight," he said. "By the way, my name is Ernesto."

Ana left the immigration office not knowing what to do. After a short walk, she decided to take a bus to Parque Copelia, located at the Vedado neighborhood, near 23rd Street and L Avenue. A cup of ice cream would do her good, as she was not in the mood for a proper lunch.

She stood in line for a long while, distracting herself by examining the people around her, telling herself how overdressed she was, as most women wore t-shirts, short pants, and sandals. When her turn arrived, she bought a scoop of vanilla ice cream and sat at the counter. She ate it slowly, hoping each tablespoon would somehow help clear her thoughts. But the place was packed and noisy, not the ideal setting to clear her mind. Once she had consumed it, thoughts exploded in her head, too numerous to unravel.

She told herself to return home and forget about the whole thing, but after waiting at the bus stop for a while, she began to walk towards Copelia Park again. She strolled around the park for a while, watching the other families pass by, focusing on a couple with a boy and a girl. Then sadness came over her.

She left the park when the sun was setting on the horizon, and a glow of gold bathed every tree around her but not before utilizing the public bathroom to wash her face and freshen up. Thirty minutes later, she found herself knocking on a door at a Vedado apartment. Ernesto opened, wearing a white undershirt and a pair of blue pants. For a moment, he stared at her in a lecherous way and let her in.

"I'm glad you could make it," he said. Then he looked in either direction before closing the door.

"Please sit," he said, pointing to the sofa.

She obeyed as her hands turned cold. To distract herself, she looked around the apartment. It was small and furnished with a black leather sofa and a round table with two chairs. Illuminated by the glow of two lamps on either side, it looked like the apartment of a single man, with boxing picture frames, nude women in suggestive poses.

"Make yourself at home," he said. "I'll get you a drink."

"I didn't come here to drink," she replied.

"Just some rum and punch," he said, rubbing his chin. "Come on, I made it just for you."

She thought about it. Perhaps a drink would take the edge off, but she didn't have a chance to say anything. He walked toward the back of the apartment and returned with two glasses. He offered one to her, sat next to her, and took a sip from his.

"Please drink," he said. "I hope it's not too sweet."

She obeyed. It was sweet, cold, and not too strong. In fact, she found it rather refreshing. She was thirsty from the long walk, so she drank it fast, and then placed the empty glass on the coffee table. He had been watching her drink it with a smirk on his face.

"Would you like another?" he asked.

"No, one is enough," she said. "Look I won't be here long. I just came to talk."

He didn't say anything, just stared at her, his eyes focused on her bosom.

"You're very beautiful," he said, sliding his fingers over her bare arm. "And I think we can help each other."

She stood abruptly, realizing at that moment something wasn't right.

"I don't feel well," she said, holding on to the sofa. She felt faint and the room was spinning. Her inquisitive eyes tried to find his. Then unclear memories scrambled in her head: him reaching under her dress, her trying to fight him but not finding the strength. She remembered slurring her words to make him stop. Her eyes closed and when they opened again, she felt him inside her, his handkerchief stuffed in her mouth, her hands tied to the bed rails. She tried to move, but it felt as if she were watching herself from outside her own body. She recalled his hands ascending from her elbows to her shoulders, and then to her breasts. She could not remember anything after that.

Later, when she awoke again, she noticed he was sitting on a chair near the bed in his underwear, watching her. Her hands were free now, but her wrists hurt, and when she tried to massage them, she noticed all of her clothes had been removed. She reached for the sheets and covered herself, and as her alertness started to return, she felt the moisture between her legs, the soreness. Once again the broken memories of what had happened emerged choppy, scattered.

"What happened?" she asked. "What did you do?" When he didn't respond, she closed her eyes and rubbed her forehead. "My head hurts," she said.

"It was just a drink," Ernesto replied.

"What did you put in it?"

"Nothing," he said. "You started to take your clothes off, and the rest is history."

"Where are my clothes?" she shouted.

"Don't raise your voice. It won't help you."

"Give me my clothes, you son-of-a-bitch!" she screamed.

"No need to get mean," he said. He picked up her clothes off the floor and threw them on the bed. "I told you I could help you, but everything has a price," he added with an apathetic tone that disturbed her.

Never had Ana met someone with so much darkness within. Now everything she'd thought about herself had shattered into pieces. How little she knew about the world. Her father had pampered her until the very end. Then her husband treated her like his most valued possession, like a piece of fine glass, perpetuating the flawed concept she had about life and other human beings. Also, until now, her husband had been the only man in her life. In one day, Ernesto had destroyed everything she held dear.

Her hands had turned ice cold again. She looked around the room trying to find a clock, wondering how long she had been asleep. "Can you leave, so I can get dressed?"

"There's nothing I haven't seen already," he replied. "No need to be shy."

She reached for her panties first and began to get dressed under the sheets.

"Come on," he said. "No need to be rude."

He pulled the sheets off her, and her clothes fell on the floor.

"This is more like it," he said

Dressed in only her panties, she sprang out of the bed and picked up her clothes. After she had clasped her bra, he walked up to her. She stepped back until she reached the wall, and while trying to push him off of her, he fondled her breasts. "Get away from me!" she yelled, fighting him off until she managed to free herself and step away. "You're filthy!" she blared out, fuming.

He grinned but didn't pursue her. "You don't have to be so angry at me, mamacita."

She reached for her dress and slipped it on.

"I shouldn't have come," she said. "Is this what you do, you son-of-a-bitch? And you think this makes you a man? All along, you had no plans of helping my family, right? This is all a big joke to you!"

He smirked. "But I have every intention of helping you, mamacita," he said blocking the door and looking at her up and down. "I really do."

"Coming here was a horrible mistake," she said.

He responded with a derisive laughter.

"Mistake?" he asked. "This is no mistake. You knew what would happen, but don't get me wrong. I'm not complaining."

The more he spoke, the more her anger built up inside.

"I'll report you," she said choking in her tears.

"Report me?" he asked and laughed with sarcasm. "Who do you think they are going to believe, you, a filthy *gusana*, a traitor to the country, or me? You are everything this government hates."

She stared at him, repulsed by him and everything he represented, realizing the validity of his words.

"I need to go home," she said.

He laughed and stepped out of her way.

"Don't worry about anything, and remember these things take time, mi amor," he said. "Come back this weekend, and I'll give you an update on your case. You really don't think one time is enough to repay such a big favor, do you?"

She reached for her purse and dashed out of the bedroom and out of the apartment. Laughing, he watched her leave.

It was dark when she went out on the street, and most of the people were inside their homes. The street smelled like jasmines and coffee, but she reeked of him. The thought of his hands on her body sickened her. What now?

Realizing she couldn't return home in her condition, Ana took a bus to her mother's house. As she stood on the crowded bus, holding on to a metal bar above her, she felt the eyes of the people burying into her. They must have noticed her hair in disarray, the smell of sweat and sex emanating from her, the shame in her eyes. The thought of keeping what had happened from her husband sickened her, but the last thing she needed was a confrontation between Ernesto and him. If her husband knew, he would kill Ernesto and end up in jail or in front of the *paredón*.

She didn't know what time it was when she arrived at her mother's apartment. It was late, and she used her key to go in, thinking her mother and aunt slept, but instead, she found them watching television with the lights off. It took all she had to conceal her tears when her mother and aunt embraced her and kissed her in front of the glow of the television set.

They were watching the black and white movie *Gentlemen Prefer Blondes.* After lowering the volume, they inundated her with questions about her trip to immigration. They also wanted to know why she had arrived so late. Her husband had stopped by when she didn't get home. He was worried. Ana didn't say much, other than her trip had been unfruitful. She had stopped at a friend's house, but when she was on the bus—she told them—her period came early, so she wanted to shower before going home. Without suspecting anything, her aunt opened a new pack of women's underwear she had received from the United States and gave her one.

Ana stepped inside the tub and, as the water fell over her body, she scrubbed herself with a small wash cloth vigorously until she felt pain. The more she scrubbed her skin, the angrier she became, until she burst into tears. She cried in silence for a long time until her tears stopped flowing. When she finished bathing, she stood in front of the mirror. Her face was red. She applied makeup to disguise the redness. As she was getting dressed, the electricity went off, and she stood in the middle of the bathroom in the dark.

"Ana, are you okay?" her aunt asked from the other side moments later. She could see a glow from a candle underneath the door.

"Yes," she answered.

"Here's a lantern you can use."

With the help of the lantern, Ana finished getting dressed and left.

Chapter 8

The streets were dark, with only the light from an occasional kerosene lamp illuminating some of the front porches of the houses in her path. She could hear the voices from the neighbors who had gathered on their porches or balconies to converse, but she couldn't see them. It was better that way. She wanted to disappear from the face of the earth.

Her husband was still awake when she arrived. He and Amanda sat in rocking chairs in the front porch, accompanied by the faint light of a candle. He too inundated her with questions, and she made up lies she had fabricated on the way home. She was glad he couldn't see her face when she responded.

"Do you think there's hope?" he asked.

"Of course," she assured him and kissed him on the cheek. "Don't worry. I'll take care of everything." But she didn't say this with the assertiveness she had displayed in previous occasions.

He held her hand, making her wonder if he would notice how cold it was.

"Come on," he said. "Sit next to me."

She sat in a rocking chair by her husband and daughter, and the three stayed there for a while. When it became evident the electricity wouldn't return that evening, he suggested they go to bed. After they found themselves alone, lying next to each other, he turned towards her and embraced her.

"Sorry for being angry before," he said. "I missed you."

"I missed you too," she said with a numb voice.

He made love to her that night with the desperation of a lover, and although she felt nothing, she couldn't give herself away. She had to make him believe she was still alive, when in reality, she felt dead inside. Faking her desperation for him, she moaned and buried her fingers into his skin, all along trying to convince herself life was still worth living. Later, after he screamed in ecstasy, she asked herself how she would be able to conceal what had occurred.

Before he fell asleep, he asked again:

"Are you sure your plans will work?"

"I hope so," she said, staring at the ceiling. "I'll do everything it takes."

CHAPTER 9

Arturo and his wife were watching the evening news when he jolted off the couch and stood in front of her. "I can't stand watching these people protest about the war," he said. Then, while pointing up with his index finger, he added: "You know who's to blame for what's happening in this country?"

She shook her head slowly from side to side and gave him a blank stare.

"It's the communists!" he said, waving his hands up in the air in anger and tensing his body. "We have to be careful, you know, or soon, we'll have another Castro in the White House."

The Vietnam War and the protests around the country dominated the evening news. The country was divided between "The New Right," which favored conservative family values, and those of the left, fighting for equality and against the war. Arturo had experienced this division within his own household when his daughter marched in an anti-war protest in the late 1960s in New York, another reason for his deep-seated disappointment.

Chapter 9

From the dining room, where Rodolfo studied, he could hear his uncle talking about the state of the country while the news played in the background. At the conclusion of a heated monologue, Arturo walked towards the television set and turned it off.

"Enough!" he shouted. "I refuse to watch these communists trying to destroy this country."

Arturo then stormed past the dining room without saying a word, and moments later, Rodolfo heard him slamming the door. Martica stayed in the living room, but after a while, she got off the couch and joined Rodolfo in the dining room.

"I don't know why he turns on the news," she whispered to Rodolfo. "It upsets him too much."

Rodolfo smiled, and before he could reply to her, he heard the telephone ring. Martica rushed towards it. After greeting the caller, she remained silent for a while.

"Oh no!" she said, followed by another long silence and a third one after "Dear God!"

"I am so sorry," she said and took a deep breath. "I will tell him."

When the call ended, Martica glanced at Rodolfo but didn't say anything.

"Is everything okay?" he asked without lifting his eyes from his work.

"Yes," she responded with a slight shrug of her shoulders. "But let me leave you alone so you can study."

She didn't wait for his response and disappeared in the back of the house.

Chapter 9

He was still working on his homework—his books spread over the dining table—when his uncle and his aunt reappeared, sat across from him, and waited to get his attention.

He put down his pen and glanced at them.

"Is everything okay?" he asked.

"We need to talk, son," said his uncle.

Rodolfo turned his head towards his aunt and noticed her reddened face and eyelashes clumped together. He patted her on the back.

"What's wrong, Tía Martica?"

"We have something important to tell you," said Arturo. "It's about your parents."

"Are they okay?"

"Yes," answered Arturo. "But let me get to the point. You know I don't like to beat around the bush. Your aunt and I wanted to surprise you. I had gathered the money for the visas, paid the attorney for the paperwork, and sent the visas to Havana, but we received a call from your mom today."

Rodolfo looked at his uncle with a furrowed brow while Arturo took a long, deep breath.

"That mother-fucker!" he yelled and slammed the table with his fists.

"Who?" asked Rodolfo.

"Fidel Castro. Who else?" he replied.

"What did he do?"

"Son, your parents won't be able to leave Cuba," said Arturo. "Castro isn't allowing them or anyone else to leave."

Rodolfo put down his pencil.

"But why? Why does he care who leaves?"

Chapter 9

"I don't know why, but at the pace people were leaving Cuba... it wouldn't be long before the entire country would be in Miami. Who knows?"

Rodolfo remained quiet for a moment, but the silence was interrupted by Martica's outburst of emotions.

"It's not fair," she said. Her voice cracked and caught in her throat. "It's not fair to separate children from their parents. I'm so sorry, nephew."

"Martica, stop crying," said her husband. "We'll figure something out."

Rodolfo looked down and stretched his fingers backwards, one at a time, while many thoughts rushed through his mind.

"I need to go for a walk," he said, rising from his chair. "I'll be back later."

His aunt tried to go after Rodolfo, but Arturo grabbed her arm.

"Leave him alone," he said.

***

It was dark outside. Rodolfo didn't know where he was going at first, but he needed to get away from the house and breathe some fresh air. The Little Havana neighborhood, named by its Cuban residents, looked cozier at night. It was a place with its own rhythm and soul. Those who had left Cuba to come here had infused it with a unique *savor*, one not found anywhere else in the world. Rodolfo could drink a café con leche, have a guava pastry, enjoy a coconut ice cream cone, watch men play dominoes in the park, and reminisce about Cuba at a family-owned cafeteria, all within a one-mile stretch. Passing by a number of homes, many with small front porches, some with shingled, gable roofs, and others with flat roofs, Rodolfo thought about all the dreams that would now have to be placed on hold. So many times, he had passed by these houses, hoping to see his parents in one of them one day.

As he walked, he saw a few people sitting outside, speaking in Spanish, but unlike in Cuba, he hardly knew any of his neighbors. Except for friends Martica had made through the years, everyone minded their own business and focused on their own families, so different than in Cuba where everyone knew other people's affairs. That made him feel lonely sometimes but never more than at this moment.

People in Little Havana had installed a memory of Cuba in every corner, from a statue of the Virgin of Charity in a garden, to a post of a Cuban flag, to a tall queen palm tree or a flamboyant tree, as if deep down, they had come to the realization they would never be back. So a piece of Cuba had to come with them.

After clearing his head a little, Rodolfo thought about Lissy. He consulted his watch under a street lamp. It was 8:30. Then, without much thought, he began to walk in the direction of her house.

When he arrived, the lights on the front porch were off, but he could see movement inside the house. He pressed the bell and waited. Moments later, Sara opened the door.

Chapter 9

"Hi," she said with a welcoming smile. "What a surprise! Lissy didn't say you were coming, but please come in."

"I didn't tell her I was coming," he replied. "I just need to talk to her for a moment, and if you don't mind, I'd rather stay on the porch."

"Is everything okay?"

He hesitated for a moment. "Yes. Everything is fine."

"Sit on one of those rocking chairs, and I'll let her know you're here."

A couple of minutes later, the lights on the front porch came on and Lissy appeared. Her mother stayed by the door, watching the teenagers. When her daughter noticed it, she turned her head toward her.

"We'll be fine, Mom," she said. "I'll be right in."

"I'll be inside if you need anything," Sara said.

Sara went back inside, leaving the door slightly open, but Lissy approached it and pulled the handle towards her without shutting it all the way. She then turned to Rodolfo and whispered: "She's always listening to my conversations."

He forced a smile.

"Is everything okay?" she asked, as if noticing his somber expression.

He shook his head, and she pushed a rocking chair close to his and sat down.

"What's wrong? Do you want to talk about it?"

He remained in silence for a while until he responded: "It's my parents."

"What happened?"

Once he began to explain what had occurred, she covered her mouth with her hand.

"Oh my God!" she said.

"My dad will be so pissed off about all this," he replied. "I know it. He didn't want me to leave, and now..."

He took a deep breath. Lissy rose off her rocking chair, pushed it aside, and grabbed him by his hands.

"Come here," she said, pulling him out of his seat." Let's go to the park, so we can have more privacy."

He followed her to the sidewalk, and they began to walk away from the house, towards 13th Avenue.

"Things will get better," she said. "Don't worry."

Rodolfo didn't respond, and to distract him, she began to talk about a variety of topics. Even though he nodded or acknowledged her in some way, his mind wandered elsewhere. After walking for a while, they arrived at a park that was several blocks long, with few people walking under the canopy of its *ceiba* trees. Rows of houses lined the street on both sides of the park.

"Have you been here before?" she asked.

He shook his head.

"I love this park. My mom used to bring me here as a child. It holds many memories."

"I'm sorry I'm not the best friend to have around this evening," he said. "I wasn't expecting this. It's not me I'm worried about. I'm a man and can take care of myself, but I'm worried about my family."

"What are you worried about?"

"Mom acts strong, like nothing can stop her, but deep down, she's fragile. Dad will be angry, but he'll be okay. Then, there's my little sister and my grandmother. It could be years before I see them again."

"At least that's better than *never* having the possibility of seeing them."

"What do you mean?" he asked.

She looked down and became reflective. After a moment of quiet reflection, she raised her head and their eyes met.

"Do you want to know what happened to my father?" she asked.

Rodolfo looked at her with a perplexed expression but remained silent.

"I think it's time to tell you," she said. "Let's sit down first. My feet hurt."

He followed her to the nearest park bench and sat next to her. An old man passed by, pulling a white terrier, and said *buenas noches* to them. Lissy and Rodolfo returned the greeting and waited for him to be a few steps away before continuing their conversation.

"I was a child when armed guards came to my house and took him away like a common criminal," Lissy said. She looked at the sky for a moment, then her eyes focused on Rodolfo. "But my father was no criminal. His only crime was he disagreed with Castro's government and what it did to the country."

She paused for a moment, her eyes filling with tears as she tilted her head.

"And you know what happened?" she asked. "I never saw him again. Not alive anyways. Mom thought I was sleeping, but when I heard her crying and screaming, I opened the door of my bedroom and peeked out just in time to see my father. He was shot in the head in front of the television cameras, and I saw when his body hit the ground."

She choked as she said the last words and broke into sobs. He sat closer to her and placed his arm around her.

"I'm sorry, I didn't know," he said and patted her shoulder. "Come on. Don't cry."

She bowed her head as her tears kept falling, making him feel helpless. Lissy's revelation made him appreciate her more than ever before. What a burden for her to carry all those years. He now understood, more than ever, why his mother had taken him out of Cuba. While absorbed in his thoughts, he kept patting Lissy on her back. For a moment, he thought about kissing her, hoping to take her sadness away, but when the memories of the night at her relative's wedding returned, he didn't. After a while, she stopped crying and took a deep breath.

"I'm sorry," she said. "That's why I don't like talking about my dad or Cuba. It makes me too upset. I didn't mean to make this about me. You have the right to be hurt and angry." She paused for a moment and reached for his hand. "My mom says hope is the last thing we should lose. Who knows? Maybe Castro will be overthrown one day, and you could go back to visit."

He looked at her but didn't say anything. Her hand remained on his for a moment, then she retrieved it and stretched her fingers.

"We need to get back," she said. "Mom will be worried and upset. I didn't tell her I was leaving. Besides, she always tells me: 'Don't go anywhere alone with a boy. Decent girls don't do that.'" She said the last two sentences mocking her mother.

He giggled. "You *do* sound like her, but she's right, you know? You're too nice and someone may take advantage."

"You're not one of those guys who takes advantage of nice girls, are you?" she asked, crossing her arms. "Besides, I can take care of myself."

"Wow! I'm *so* scared," he said with a derisive laugh.

She gave him a little push, followed by "Hey! Stop making fun of me!" and more laughter filling the empty streets. As they walked back, he felt relieved and appreciative of Lissy's ability to listen and comfort him. Her strength in the face of adversity gave him strength.

When he and Lissy arrived at her house, Sara was on the front porch, leaning over the chest-high wall separating it from the street.

"Lissy, I was worried sick!" Sara said frantically. "Where were you? Why didn't you say you were leaving?"

Lissy apologized and looked down.

Chapter 9

"We'll talk about it later," Sara said. Then her eyes focused on Rodolfo. "Mijo, your aunt called a few minutes ago. You need to go home right away. It's urgent."

"What happened?" he asked.

"It's your uncle," Sara said. "Your aunt called the ambulance. They are on their way."

"An ambulance?" he asked. "Why? What happened?"

"Your aunt was talking too fast. It was hard to understand her, but I thought she mentioned something about his heart."

Lissy and Rodolfo exchanged glances.

"Can I go with him, Mom?" asked Lissy.

"No, you can't!" Sara said. "Tomorrow is a school day, and you need to keep those grades up."

"But Mom!" Lissy protested.

"Don't worry, Lissy," he said. "I'll call you later."

He kissed her on the cheek.

"See you tomorrow," he said. "Good night, Ms. O'Donnell."

"Good night," said Sara. "Please call us and tell us how he's doing. If there is anything you need, let me know."

Rodolfo rushed home and arrived as the paramedics were taking his uncle out of the house on a stretcher. Martica rushed to her nephew and embraced him.

"I'm so glad you're here!" she said.

Arturo lay still, his face sweaty and reddened.

"What happened?" he asked.

"I'll explain on the way to the hospital. It's best if we follow the ambulance. At first, I wanted to ride with him, but the paramedics suggested I drive. I'm so shaken."

"I can drive, Tía Martica."

"You know how?" she asked.

"Yes, Tío has given me a few lessons, and I have my restricted license. Where are they taking him?"

"Jackson Memorial. Here's the key. Let's hurry."

On the way to the hospital, Martica was inconsolable.

"Tía, what happened?" Rodolfo asked, looking at the road, both hands on the steering wheel. "He was fine before I left. I don't understand."

Martica choked back the tears as she described what happened. "He wasn't fine," she said and took a deep breath. "He was acting. You know how he is, playing tough, but he really isn't the person he claims to be. He cares too much. That's his problem. There are things he has gone through you don't know, and I'd rather not say. Those things turned him into who he is. Also, his constant preoccupation with money... I told him I could get a job. He won't allow it, so he tries to save every penny. After spending money for the attorneys and the visas for your family, and then learning they couldn't leave, he felt he had wasted all those savings that could've been used for your education. He was so angry. And then, not being to help his sister. It's too much for him."

Chapter 9

"Tía, he doesn't need to worry so much. I promise to pay back every cent he spent on my parents and me."

"It's not that. You don't understand." She shook her head, and glanced at him with a look of concern. "He wants to be a good provider and doesn't like asking anyone for help. He's stubborn like your grandfather used to be. May God bless his soul. I'm so scared! If something were to happen to Arturo, I don't know what I would do."

"He'll be fine. I'm sure. But... what was he feeling?"

"He had shortness of breath and complained of chest pain. I thought he was having a heart attack, so I called the ambulance and our daughter. She's a nurse, you know? She also thinks it's his heart. Arturo and our daughter fight so much with each other... for silly things, but when I told her what was going on, she burst into tears. They're more alike than they think. She told me she would take a flight to Miami tomorrow morning. "

"I can sleep on the sofa, so she can take my room," said Rodolfo.

"You don't have to do that."

"I want to."

Instead of contradicting him, Martica changed the topic.

"With so much going on, I didn't ask you how you were doing... about the latest news," she said. "Where did you go? You scared me."

Rodolfo shook his head.

"Don't worry about me, Tía. I was upset and needed a walk. Then, I stopped by Lissy's house."

"Are the two of you...?" she asked opening her eyes wide.

"No, we're just good friends. That's all."

"I guess I'm getting old and don't understand young people today. She's a nice girl, you know. I like her."

"I know," Rodolfo replied. "But my life is a little complicated between schoolwork, my job, and improving my English."

Martica raised her eyebrows, as if the maturity and conviction in his words had impressed her.

"Listen, about your parents," she said. "You can stay at our house as long as you need. We will help you with college expenses."

"No, Tía. I have a job. Lissy tells me I can apply for financial aid. I don't want to be a burden. You and Tío need to take care of yourselves. It's enough you're giving me a place to live."

"You are as hard-headed as your uncle."

He smiled and talked to her about his plans after high school. A classmate told him he needed to sign up for military service and apply for an educational deferral. Rodolfo didn't mind going to Vietnam, but he hoped to finish his education before his deployment. Martica agreed.

"I wouldn't want you to go to war," she said. "I've grown to love you like a son, and I wouldn't want anything to happen to you."

Martica tapped his shoulder a couple of times, and he replied with a smile.

Chapter 9

After Rodolfo's and Martica's arrival at Jackson Memorial, it took almost two hours before she was allowed to join Arturo. The doctor came to speak to her some time later and confirmed Arturo had suffered a mild heart attack. After that, she refused to leave Arturo's side, even after the doctors transferred him to the intensive care unit, where a nurse assured her Arturo would receive the best care. But Martica had seen fear in her husband's eyes when he looked around the room and at the equipment hooked up to him. No one would convince her to go home that evening and leave him when he needed her the most.

Rodolfo was able to join Martica and Arturo for a while. After midnight, despite her concern Rodolfo could be caught by police driving that late with a restricted license, she asked Rodolfo to go back home and sleep for a few hours. He needed to be at the airport early to pick up his cousin.

CHAPTER 10

Rodolfo's sign displaying his cousin's name, Clara, made it easy for her to find him in the crowd of friends and family waiting for arriving passengers. When he first saw her, he didn't think she looked much like the picture he had seen of her in his bedroom, especially her hair, colored blond now and held back in a ponytail. Her brown eyes resembled her father's, and not only was she taller than her mother, but she had a thin, fit body, like those of women who ran in New York City's Central Park. She wore an unassuming pair of dark blue jeans and a black t-shirt.

When she noticed him, she rushed towards him displaying a big smile—as if she had known him for years—and gave him a hug.

"You must be cousin Rodolfo," she said with a cheerful smile.

He nodded and reached for her luggage.

"Wow!" she said. "Mom said you looked like my brother, but I never thought... Oh my God. The resemblance is so remarkable."

He looked at her with inquisitive eyes.

"You have a brother?"

She shook her head and repositioned her carryon luggage.

"He passed away a few years" ago," she explained.

"I'm sorry," he said. "I didn't know. How old was he?"

"About your age," she said. They started to walk towards the exit slowly. Rodolfo was confused. In all the time he had been at the house, neither Martica nor Arturo had talked about their son. "His death hit Dad hard. My brother was his favorite child, his pride and joy... Anyhow. That's in the past. How's Dad?"

"He's stable. Do you want me to take you to the house first?

"No," she said. "Let's go straight to the hospital. I'd like to see him."

Later, as Rodolfo drove to the hospital in the middle of rush-hour traffic, he noticed his cousin's melancholic look as she looked at the people around her.

"I miss this place," she said. "These are my people, you know. New York is so different. I love the city. Don't get me wrong. But there's something about Miami I can't explain. Maybe it's that I feel closer to my roots here."

"I haven't been to New York City, but I hear there are a lot more Cubans in Miami than up there. You miss this place so much because Miami's your home."

"Talking about home. I heard what happened to your parents. Do you miss them? Do you miss your home in Cuba?"

He took a deep breath. "Clara, right?" He looked at her for a brief moment and then his eyes focused on the road.

She nodded.

"Let me explain," he said. "It's complicated. I don't like to dwell on things. I'm not going to tell you I don't miss my parents or Cuba, but I prefer to live in the present and think about the future."

"A defense mechanism," she said.

"Defense? Against what?"

"Your true feelings," she said.

He smiled. "I get it. I see what you're trying to do. But it's not going to work, cousin. I may not be like Uncle Arturo—who doesn't want me to call him Uncle, by the way—and keeps everything inside, but I'm a man. Men handle situations as they come and don't feel sorry for themselves."

"Did your father teach you that?"

"He did."

She laughed.

"I like you," she said, tucking her hair behind her ear. "And now I see why Dad doesn't want to get close to you."

"Clara, you seem to enjoy psychoanalyzing everyone" he said. "Are you sure nursing is your calling?"

"You're not the only one who has said that to me. I used to drive my father crazy."

"So tell me. Why doesn't your dad want to get close to me? Am I a bad guy?"

"No. It's your resemblance to my brother. Losing him was the hardest test he had to face since he left Cuba."

Chapter 10

They remained in silence for a moment, while Rodolfo thought about what Clara had said.

"Are you hungry?" she asked.

"I'm starving. I didn't eat anything before I left the house because I didn't want to be late."

She smiled. "I'll take you to one of my favorite places in Miami," she said. "You'll like it."

She began to give him directions until they stopped in front of La Carreta. They ordered café con leche, Cuban toast, and eggs before resuming their journey to the hospital, all along, their conversation staying as animated as before.

"It's weird, you know," she said as they walked towards the cardiac intensive care unit of Jackson Memorial Hospital. "Mom always says there's nothing like family. She's right. You feel so familiar to me, never mind the fact you look so much like my brother. I feel I can talk to you about anything, like a brother."

He smiled.

"I feel the same way about you and your mom," he replied.

"What about Dad?"

"He has been difficult to figure out. Until now."

"I have a surprise for him," Clara said. "Actually two surprises, but don't ask me what they are. I want to tell everyone at the same time."

Rodolfo stared at her with a playful inquisitive expression. "Don't keep looking at me that way," she said. "It won't work."

When the cousins arrived at the unit, they learned Arturo had been transferred to a regular room.

"That's a good sign," said Clara.

The two cousins arrived to the room a couple of minutes before Arturo, accompanied by his wife, rolled in. When Martica saw Clara, she rushed to her with open arms and eyes full of tears. "Thank you for flying down to see your dad, Clarita," she said. "I've been so scared."

"Let's stop all that worrying, Martica," Arturo said grumpily. "It's nothing. I'll be fine."

After kissing and embracing her mother, Clara approached her father with a loving smile. She waited for the healthcare workers to place him on the bed and leave the room before she kissed him on the cheek.

"How are you, Dad?" she asked.

He waved his arm. "I told you I'm fine. Nothing to worry about. You know your mother, always making a big deal about everything."

"I missed you, mi viejito. I missed you so much."

Arturo swallowed and turned his head away from his daughter as his eyes became moist.

"Mom, sit down," she said, touching her father's bed. "Dad, can I get you some water?"

"The doctor doesn't want me to drink anything until all the tests are done."

"More tests?" Martica asks. "I thought they were done. Isn't that what the nurse said?"

"No, that's not what she said," Arturo answered.

"Okay, the two of you stop acting like a married couple," Clara said, giggling. "I guess some things never change. Let's all relax and talk about more pleasant news."

Martica, Rodolfo, and Clara sat around the bed, Clara very close to her parents, and Rodolfo towards his uncle's feet.

"Should I step out, so you and your parents can speak with more privacy?" Rodolfo asked.

Clara crossed her arms and gave her cousin an inquisitive look. "Are you serious, Rodolfo? First, you're family. Second, I already told you that I've only known you for less than two hours, and I feel as if my brother were back."

Arturo looked away when his daughter finished her last sentence while Martica reached for Rodolfo's hand and placed her between hers. "Sweetheart," she said with the shine of her emotions appearing in her eyes. "Now, you're our son too."

"Thank you, Tía Martica," Rodolfo said, rubbing his forehead.

"Now that we've established how much everyone in this room loves each other, let's get to the news. No more interruptions." She paused for a moment and looked at her father with glistening eyes. "I know it's been hard for you and Mom to be without me for the past few years. I hope you understand that after my brother died, I needed to find myself. I couldn't stay here, Dad. But my life is finally what I hoped it would be. I'm a nurse manager. I have a loving husband, and we've matured as a couple. Therefore, we've decided it's time to come back home."

Martica jumped out of her seat. "You're coming back to Miami?" she asked and embraced her daughter. "Oh my God. I've prayed so much for this moment."

"Mom," said Clara. "Please sit a little longer. There's more."

Martica obeyed, but her legs kept shaking from the excitement.

"What about the property you own?" Her mother asked.

"We listed it for sale," she said. "We'll need to move in with you for a little while after it sells, so we can find a place in Miami. Would that be okay?"

"Of course that's okay," Martica said without waiting for her husband to respond. Realizing her husband's preference to be the decision-maker, she turned to him. "Do you agree, mi amor? At last, we can have our daughter at home!"

He nodded, and his wife kissed him on the cheek.

"I could sleep on the sofa," Rodolfo offered. "This way my cousin will have her room back."

"No need for that," said Clara. "Dad, could you give up your 'Cuba' Room?"

"Cuba Room?" asked Rodolfo.

Clara glanced at her father, waiting for him to respond, but when she noticed his discomfort, she replied to her cousin.

"Dad converted my brother's room into his personal all-things Cuba shrine."

Arturo waved his hand at her.

"I can store all that old stuff in boxes," Arturo said. "The way things are in Cuba, we're most likely never going back, so what's the point?"

"I think that's true, especially after I tell you the next news, Dad," Clara said.

"Can you stop with all your secrets and mystery and tell us once and for all?" Arturo said with a sullen look.

"Fine, Dad," Martica replied with a smile. "I will tell you. I need you to get healthy soon because you'll need a lot of energy to run after your grandchild. That's the news, you grumpy man. You're going to be an abuelo."

Arturo's eyes filled with tears, and as much as he tried to hold them back, they rolled down his face. Seeing her father cry broke Clara's heart.

"Oh Dad," she said, rising from the bed and throwing herself in her father's arms, her head resting on his chest. "I didn't mean to make you cry."

Martica joined them in their embrace, her eyes full of happy tears, which left Rodolfo feeling awkward.

"Rodolfo!" Clara said, lifting her head, as if she had noticed his nervousness. "What are you waiting for? Stop acting like my dad. It's family-hug time."

They all embraced, cried, and smiled until a nurse, who had entered the room and noticed everyone crying, asked: "Tissues, anyone?"

CHAPTER 11

Once Arturo left the hospital, Martica waited until he was recovered before reminding him they needed to clear the Cuba Room to make space for Rodolfo.

"I don't want you to strain yourself," she said, touching his hand. "Rodolfo and I will help you."

"I don't need anyone to help me," he replied. "I'll do it myself."

As the days and weeks passed, Arturo seemed to stay in the Cuba Room longer than before, until one day when his daughter announced her house had been sold and she and her husband were driving to Miami with some of their belongings. They had sold or given to charity everything else. All of a sudden, getting the room ready became an emergency, and Arturo had no choice but to accept Rodolfo's help.

Rodolfo's anticipation grew. At last, he would be able to step inside this restricted area of the house. He had never heard anyone refer to it as the "Cuba Room," neither had he placed a foot inside it. It required a key to gain access and, as far as he knew, it was always locked. He had checked a few times, out of curiosity. Only his uncle appeared to have the key. Arturo entered it often and stayed there an hour at a time. Martica would go on about her chores and, by the time he exited the room, she had a cup of café con leche ready for him. It was a routine he seemed to appreciate, judging by the way he caressed her shoulder when he returned his empty cup to her. Rodolfo found it strange that not many words had to be exchanged between them for people to realize how much they meant to each other.

When the day of the Cuba Room cleaning arrived, Rodolfo tried to conceal his excitement about discovering what was in it.

"Don't touch anything unless I tell you," Arturo warned Rodolfo before opening the door.

Rodolfo nodded in agreement and followed his uncle inside with careful steps, almost as if he were stepping into a museum or a church. What he saw impressed him more than it shocked him. So many pictures on the wall, some black and white and some in color. It was the first time Rodolfo had seen pictures of his dead cousin, and he couldn't believe the similarities. He could've been his twin brother. The pictures had been arranged by year, making it easy for people to watch the boy grow before their eyes. Two walls were dedicated to him and the other two to Cuba. Rodolfo saw detailed maps of the island and of Havana, pictures of the Morro Fort and the Capitolio building, and a blown-up stamp of the Virgin of Charity.

A bed with a single mattress, covered by a blue and white bedspread, rested against the wall on one side of the small room.

Rodolfo scratched his head.

"Are you sure you want to box all these pictures?" Rodolfo asked. "I don't mind if you leave the room as is. I don't spend too much time in my room anyway. I only go there to sleep."

Arturo looked at Rodolfo for a moment with a surprised look. "Are you sure you wouldn't mind leaving it like this?"

"Of course not!" Rodolfo replied, looking at his uncle. At that moment, Rodolfo noticed the drops of perspiration gathering on his uncle's forehead.

"Let me think about it," Arturo said, moving his eyebrows closer together. "Let's box the clothes in the closet and the bedding..." Arturo paused, took a deep breath, and brought his hand to his chest. "Actually, I need some fresh air. Let me have Martica help you with that."

Arturo had turned pale.

"Why don't you sit down, Arturo," Rodolfo said. "Let me bring you some water."

"I don't need anything!" Arturo said and stormed out of the room.

Rodolfo stayed in the room, afraid to touch anything. He was about to go look for his aunt when she showed up with a couple of boxes.

"I knew it!" she said when she walked in. "This is too much for him, and now he's having chest pain."

"Tía, I don't want to inconvenience my uncle," said Rodolfo. "He has done more than enough for my family and me. I could try to work more hours and find a small place…"

"Nonsense!" Martica interrupted him. "Sit down, and let me explain something I didn't want to say before, but I think it's time."

Martica and Rodolfo sat at the end of the bed, and she placed her hand on his.

"Since you arrived into my life, it was as if God had gifted me a son." She paused for a moment and glanced at one of the pictures on the wall. "You look so much like my Fernandito, but I understood then I could not get too close to you. After all, you have your own parents, and I didn't want to get hurt again. The worst thing that can happen to parents is to have to bury their own child." Martica looked down. Moments later, she raised her head, and her eyes met Rodolfo's. "Now that your parents are not coming for who knows how long, we would be honored to do for you what we would've done for our son. I know sometimes you feel as if your uncle doesn't love you. I know he does, sweetheart, but he's afraid to love you."

"I don't understand."

"You will one day when you have your own family," she said. Her eyes once again wandered through each of the pictures, stopping on one of Fernandito and Rodolfo's mother when they were all in Cuba.

"You see that picture?" Martica asked, pointing at the wall. Rodolfo nodded. "In it are the people Arturo has loved the most in his entire life, even more than he loves me. Arturo lost them both, one to Castro's ridiculous rules. Your uncle has always been very protective of your mother. That's why he's done everything he can to help her. She's the youngest."

She shook her head and smiled.

"You know? Your uncle told me that, as a toddler, your mom cheered him *every* time he came from school. She would yell at her parents when they reprimanded Arturo, and once she even stood in front of the belt when their father tried to hit him."

She paused again and took a deep breath.

"Let's box the clothes before Arturo returns," she said hastily. "I wonder if we should paint the room and rearrange the pictures. I think it would do Arturo good."

"Don't worry. I will take care of it. Thank you for everything, Tía Martica."

Martica embraced Arturo, and he smiled and patted her on her back.

"Hey, I keep forgetting to ask you," said Martica. "How's Lissy doing?"

"She's fine," he said. "She told me she had applied to the University of Miami and a couple of other schools. She wants to be a doctor."

"I like that girl," she said. "But I'm not telling you what to do. Arturo keeps telling me to stop getting involved. I just can't help myself."

They both laugh.

"Tía Martica," Rodolfo said. "You should check on Tío Arturo."

"Yes, I should. Listen, we have some leftover paint in the storage shed from when we repainted the living room. It might still be good.

Can you go get it? You'll find paint supplies there too. Let's surprise Arturo! I will distract him."

Rodolfo spent a few hours preparing the walls and painting. Martica kept coming in and out of the room throughout the day to box her son's clothes and bedding. After consulting with her husband, she decided to donate them to charity.

Searching through her linen closet, she found a bedspread she had purchased when her son was alive but never used. Her excitement illuminated her face when she made the bed with new sheets and the new bedspread.

"I love it! Do you like it?"

"Yes, of course," said Rodolfo.

"At least I won't have to ask my little ogre for money."

Rodolfo smiled as he watched his aunt straighten the sheets, until she left them looking as perfect as those at the hotel room he had shared with his family in Costa del Sol.

The next day, Martica and Rodolfo rearranged the pictures. They placed those of Rodolfo's dead cousin on one wall, in chronological order, as they were, but closer together than before; and those of Cuba, including old maps and posters, on the parallel wall. They moved the bed to the center of the room, its head rails against the window with two pictures, one of El Morro Fort and the other of Cuba's capital building, on either side of the window.

When they were finished, Martica rushed out of the room and called her husband's name.

Chapter 11

She found him sitting in a rocking chair on the front porch, reading the newspaper.

"We have a surprise," she said.

"Does it have to be now?" he said.

"Yes. Come with me."

Reluctantly, Arturo followed her to the Cuba Room and found Rodolfo straightening one of the pictures. Arturo looked around, expressionless, concentrating on the wall where Rodolfo had arranged his son's pictures.

"Don't you like it?" asked Martica.

"Decorating the place is your department, Martica," he said and looked down. "I work and pay the bills. That's all."

Martica looped her arms through his. "But you must have an opinion, right?"

"Arturo, I'll only use this room to sleep," said Rodolfo. "During the day, you can use it as much as you like. I don't want to cause you any inconvenience. I'm thankful you're giving me a place to live."

Although Arturo didn't acknowledge his nephew's statement; he just took a deep breath, conveying relief, not anger. He then turned to his wife.

"The room is fine, Martica," Arturo said, releasing his arm from her hold.

She gave him a glowing smile and kissed him on the cheek. "I knew you would like it!" she said.

"Thank you, Rodolfo, for all the hard work," he said in a hurry, then glancing at his wife and raising his eyebrows, he added: "Can I go back to my reading now?"

Chapter 11

After she nodded in agreement, Arturo turned around and left the room.

CHAPTER 12

By the time Lissy and Rodolfo graduated from high school, Clara was six months pregnant. Clara's parents asked her to wait until the baby was born to look for another place to live. She and her husband Simon agreed, which allowed Rodolfo and Clara to deepen their friendship. On weekends, Clara, Simon, and Rodolfo enjoyed listening to records together, from *Let It Be* by the Beatles to *Bridge Over Troubled Water* by Simon & Garfunkel while they endured criticism from Arturo.

"Stop listening to that hippie music," he would say. "You know what real music is? Listen to the greats, like Benny Moré, La Sonora Matancera, and Orlando Contreras. Now, *that* was good music."

"Leave the kids alone, Arturo," Martica would tell him. "This is a different time and place."

Arturo would wave his hand in dismissal and go back to his reading.

One day, when Clara, Simon, and Rodolfo were in Clara's room listening to music, she whispered to her cousin, "Hey, do you want to see my dad dance?" She looked like a mischievous child about to do something wrong.

"Does he dance?" Rodolfo asked, opening his eyes wide. "I thought all he did was read and watch the news.

"Oh, he dances, but after my brother died, he stopped playing the music he loves. You'll see."

She walked to the record player, replaced the record she was playing with another, and placed the needle at the beginning of one of the songs. After opening the door to her room, she signaled her husband and her cousin to sit down on the bed for a moment and wait. Moments later, they heard Arturo's voice.

"Martica! Come over here. Our daughter finally learned what good music is."

They heard some steps. Clara then quietly led her cousin and her husband towards the living room, occasionally looking back and placing her index finger across her lips.

When they arrived in the living room, they saw Martica and Arturo dancing to their favorite song, *Two Gardenias for You*, the two very close to each other, and their cheeks together.

"*Dos gardenias para ti, con ellas quiero decir, te quiero*," Arturo sang in his wife's ear.

"Hey you," Clara said. "Don't get so close to each other, or I'll have to bring the hose from the backyard to spray you both."

With a dismissive wave of his hand, Arturo said to Clara: "Go away. No one called you."

"Arturo, don't be so mean to our pregnant daughter," Martica said in a loving manner.

Chapter 12

"He doesn't mean it, Mom. Let's do this, Dad. I'll join you. Simon can't dance, but I'm sure Rodolfo can. You are not a true Cuban if you can't dance. Come on, Rodolfo." Clara grabbed her cousin by the hand and joined her parents on the improvised dance floor while Simon sat down on the sofa to watch them dance. When the song was over, they all applauded and laughed.

Other than for the occasional arguments about politics or music, the family lived a cordial life, animated by the anticipation of the new baby.

Lissy and Rodolfo remained good friends, but their lives would take different paths after graduation. She had applied at the University of Miami and Florida State while Rodolfo had decided to attend the Miami Dade Community College because his English was not yet strong enough for the university setting and the cost of the university far exceeded that of the community college. As he and his uncle had discussed, he also applied for an educational deferment. This would allow him to complete his education before he had to be deployed to Vietnam or anywhere else.

During Rodolfo's first year at the community college, he spoke to his mother on a few occasions. Following the news of Castro's travel restriction, she seemed distant, as if she were hiding something. He shared his concerns with Lissy, who concluded she could be suffering from depression. Rodolfo would try to cheer his mother up by telling him about his good grades and the new baby, but nothing seemed to help.

Chapter 12

Life was changing around him. And in many ways, the world was also changing. He felt that the war had a lot to do with it. Some said the Vietnam War had eroded the innocence the people in the United States had found during the 1950s. Rodolfo's limited knowledge of that decade stemmed from the movies he and his family watched and his American History classes, yet, the transformation was palpable, even for him.

After a while, Rodolfo started dating an American girl he met in college: thin, blond-haired, blue-eyed. Not that he could count her as one of his conquests, as it was *she* who approached him. Those same characteristics he despised about himself—his shyness, lack of assertiveness, and thick accent—had sparked her interest in him.

A month after they began to date, he brought her home to introduce her to his family, a move he regretted the moment Martica and Arturo saw his girlfriend sitting on their sofa. He should have anticipated their reaction, given the way his girlfriend dressed that night: a pair of tiny white shorts and a tank top exposing her belly button that revealed her braless nipples. Not even the girl failed to notice the disapproving looks Martica and Arturo gave her. Later, as if their appalled glances had not been enough, Arturo asked Rodolfo to accompany him and Martica to the kitchen. Martica didn't waste any time.

"She's not right for you," Martica whispered. "You need a Cuban girl, like Lissy."

Arturo gave him a puzzled look, and turned his hands upwards in astonishment. "Are you on drugs or something?" he asked. "You can't possibly be in your right mind to bring *that* to a decent home like ours."

"Oh, no!" Martica said, opening her mouth wide. She then narrowed the space between her and her nephew, and pulled down the skin below his eye, a move that left Arturo even more perplexed than he already was.

"What are you doing, Martica?" Arturo asked.

"Checking if he's taking drugs," she said.

"That'll only tell you if he has anemia, not if he's taking drugs!"

They kept going back and forth for a while until Rodolfo interrupted them. "I'm not taking drugs, and I'm sorry I brought her home," Rodolfo said, waving his hands. "I don't know what I was thinking. Sorry, it won't happen again."

His girlfriend must have heard them arguing because by the time Rodolfo returned to the living room, she was gone. They would later argue, but it didn't take long for her to forgive him. She believed in free love and dressed and acted in a care-free manner, so he understood why his conservative Cuban family had found her offensive. However, she treated him with kindness and made him feel happy, especially during those nights she invited him to her room in an apartment she shared with some friends and made love to him.

Once in a while, his girlfriend would try to convince him to participate in student protests against the Vietnam War, but he preferred to be an observer. The constant scandals, plastered all over newspapers and the evening news, and the numerous protests against the Nixon administration shocked him. In Cuba, the press was controlled by the government and people couldn't openly express their disagreement with the ruling administration. Regardless of what people thought about Nixon, his uncle supported him.

"Don't listen to the media," Arturo said to him. "They lie. That's all they do. And you see all those students protesting against the war? They want a communist country. Don't listen to them, either. That's one of the reasons I don't like that girlfriend of yours. She is a commie."

"She's not, Arturo," Rodolfo said. But no one could convince Arturo otherwise. When Rodolfo tried to explain to him he was an adult and a good judge of character, Arturo would leave Rodolfo mid-sentence and lock himself in his room.

Meanwhile, tired of waiting for Rodolfo, Lissy had started to date the brother of one of her friends. Rodolfo wasn't happy when he heard about it, but he didn't feel much different than the night at the wedding. He still thought he wasn't good enough for her.

One night towards the end of his final year at the community college, Rodolfo came home distraught and sat across from his uncle. His uncle ignored him at first and kept reading the newspaper, but after a while, Arturo looked at Rodolfo from above his glasses.

"Do you have something to tell me?" Arturo asked.

Rodolfo nodded. "You were right," he said.

Chapter 12

"About?"

"My ex-girlfriend," Rodolfo said, looking down for a brief moment.

"Oh?"

"I won't go into details, but I found her with someone else."

Arturo didn't respond.

"You were right," Rodolfo reiterated with a look of disappointment on his face.

Arturo folded his paper and took off his glasses.

"Let me tell you something, son. In Cuba, we had an old saying. 'The devil knows more from experience than from being the devil,' but I will not kick you when you're down. Don't worry about it. You'll find the right girl when it's time."

Their conversation was abruptly interrupted by Clara's arrival. After finding the front door unlocked, as her parents left it on weekends when they were at home, she had entered the living room with her daughter in her arms.

"Dad, I picked up the mail!" she announced and placed several envelopes on the coffee table before she kissed her father and her cousin on the cheek.

The little girl started to cry.

"She wants the floor," said Arturo. "That or she wants her grandfather."

Clara turned to her daughter, a beautiful girl with brown, curly hair and hazel eyes.

"Do you want to go with Grandpa?"

The girl shook her head.

"Of course not," Martica said as she appeared in the living room with a big smile on her face. "She wants her grandma. Right sweetheart?"

Martica extended her arms toward her granddaughter, and the little girl reciprocated. Martica held her close and kissed her cheeks.

"I love this little pumpkin," she said. "She looks and behaves so much like her mom when she was her age."

"That explains why she doesn't like me," said Arturo.

"Don't say that, Dad! That's not true. We both love her grandfather."

"Of course, she loves her grandpa!" Martica said, speaking like a little girl and rubbing her nose against her granddaughter's. "Do you want to go with Grandpa, pretty girl? Tell Grandpa how much you love him. Here, let's try again."

Martica tried to hand the little girl to Arturo, but she began to cry with big, thick tears.

"You see?" Arturo said. "She has something against me."

Clara giggled and exchanged glances with her mother. After a few moments, the little girl began to yawn and extended her arms toward her mother. Clara took her from Martica and began to rock her.

"I think there's a letter for you in that pile, cousin," Clara said turning her eyes toward Rodolfo. "It's from the University of Miami. The envelope fell on the ground when I took the mail out of the mailbox."

Rodolfo reached for the envelopes and went through them.

Chapter 12

"That was faster than I expected," he said, taking the envelope from the university and tearing one of the ends. He read the letter, then remained quiet.

"Well..." Rodolfo said, looking at his uncle.

"Well... what?" Arturo asked.

"I did it!" Rodolfo replied with a glowing smile.

"You did what?" his uncle asked.

"I was accepted to the Electrical Engineering program at the University of Miami. I'm going to be an engineer!"

"But..." Arturo said. "I didn't know you had decided to study Engineering. You never said anything."

"I wanted to surprise you, Arturo," he said.

Arturo looked at him with a mixture of anger and confusion. Then he arose from his rocking chair, and without saying a word, he stormed out of the room, leaving Rodolfo with the letter in his hand. Perplexed, Clara followed him with her eyes, and moments later, they heard a door being slammed.

"Did I do something wrong?" asked Rodolfo. "Where did he go?"

"To the Cuba Room," Clara said. "I saw him go in."

"But why?" Rodolfo asked. "I thought he always wanted an engineer in his family. He has been saying that since the first day he saw me!"

"He did," Martica said. "You don't understand your uncle. He's happy."

"He has a strange way to show it," Clara said, rolling her eyes.

"He has a soft heart, and he doesn't believe in displaying his emotions like a flag," said Martica. "You've made your uncle very happy today. He wanted our son to be an engineer. Arturo was always telling everyone. When he died, Arturo felt useless. He had fought so hard to take his children out of Cuba to keep them safe and give them a future, but he couldn't. He then turned to Clarita, hoping *she* would make the family proud, but she went against him and became a nurse."

Clara opened her eyes wide.

"Mom, if you are going to offend me, can you wait until I leave the room?"

"It's not that, sweetheart. Now that you are a nurse manager, he's fine with your choice."

"But a nurse manager is still not as good as an engineer, is that is?" Clara said, repositioning her daughter, who was touching Clara's face with her little hands, as if noticing her frustration.

"That's not what I'm saying," Martica said. "This conversation has taken a wrong turn." She took a deep breath. "Besides, we have a lot to celebrate."

"You're right, Mom," Clara said, forcing a smile and turning toward her cousin. "Congratulations, Rodolfo. You've worked hard and deserve all the good things in life. You'll make a wonderful engineer, and I'm glad you'll be able to give my father the joy I wasn't able to give him."

Rodolfo's eyes shrank as they focused on Clara.

"Am I hearing resentment, cousin?" Rodolfo asked. "You know you're my sister, and I'll always have your back."

Clara shrugged.

"Yes, I'm a little hurt, but I'll get over it."

"Fine then," Martica said. "Family hug time."

They all embraced, while Rodolfo thought about his parents and the incomprehensiveness of their situation. It angered him he couldn't do anything to get them out of Cuba. If he attempted it, only two outcomes could result: jail or death. After almost three years in Miami, it was starting to feel like home, but at what price? His parents' life sentence in an island jail? His uncle—convinced the embargo the United States had against Cuba would work—dreamed of the day he could return to a free Cuba. He just didn't know how long it would take. But Rodolfo wasn't holding his breath.

CHAPTER 13

It had been several months since the last time Rodolfo and his mother had spoken on the telephone, and he suspected something was wrong. He shared his concerns with Martica who, through a friend of a friend, managed to locate someone in Santos Suárez who owned a telephone. Via a cablegram, Rodolfo informed Ana about the day and time he would be calling. He didn't know then that Ana no longer lived at her old address. Luckily, a person who knew where she lived delivered the news of the call to Ana.

As the day approached, Rodolfo became more anxious. He had only received a couple of letters from his mother that year, and from them, he was starting to conclude his mother was giving up. His hands turned cold as he dialed, and after a few rings, he heard her voice.

"Mamá, can you hear me? How are you? How's the family?"

"Rodolfito," she said, using the diminutive form of his name. "My good son." She slurred her words. "I miss you, like I've never missed *any*one in my life."

"Mom, is everything okay?" he asked.

"No, things are not okay. But you know what? It doesn't matter. The important thing is that you're okay."

"What's wrong? Please tell me."

"Oh no. *You* first. I'm sure there's a reason you went *out* of your way to call *me*. These calls are expensive."

"I wanted to give you the news. I graduated from the two-year college and was accepted to the electrical engineering program at the University of Miami."

She let out a hysterical laugh.

"Dear God! I can't believe it. My son, the engineer. I TOLD that father of yours that letting you go was the *right* thing to do. But nope! *Heee*... never believed me. And now, it's too late. I don't even know where he is."

"What do you mean?"

"He left me. We traded our home for two apartments, but then he moved out of *that* apartment. He took your sister with him. Actually, I told her to go with him. I'm not well, son."

His eyes filled with tears.

"What's wrong, Mamá?" he asked.

"I don't want to bother you with *my* problems. Here, write down my address."

He reached for a pen and wrote down the information his mother was giving him.

"That's the same apartment building as my grandmother," he said.

"Yes, I found a small place there."

"Mami, please take care of yourself. When I finish school and get a job, I'll visit you. I promise."

"They don't allow *anybody* to come, son. Who knows how long it will be before we see each other again, but you must go on... I'm *so* tired of fighting, of living in this damned place. I miss you and your sister so much."

"I miss you, Mom. I'll send you a package with food and anything else you need."

"Thank you, but you should save money for your studies. People tell me the university over there is expensive."

"I can get loans, and depending on my grades, I might be able to get a scholarship."

"That's good, son... My GOOD son." She paused and stayed silent for a while. "I have something important to tell you," she proceeded. "If anything ever happens to me, you need to keep going and be everything you can be. Do it for me... and for your dad. I know things didn't work out between us." She paused again and took a deep breath. "It's not his fault, you know? It's ALL mine. I tried to find a way out, but all I did was to destroy my life and your father's. He doesn't deserve this. He's a good man. I never appreciated him enough. Not until it was too late."

"I'm sure he will find his way back home," Rodolfo said. "He loves you."

"Well, son. You're spending too much on this call, hearing me talk gibberish. Spend your money wisely."

"How's Grandma and Tía?"

"They're getting older. It was not easy for them after you left."

"Tell them I'll send them good coffee, powdered milk, and chocolate."

"Aww...they'll like that. Now go, son. Congratulations!"

When Rodolfo put down the telephone, he looked at his aunt with a serious expression.

"Is everything okay?" she asked.

He shook his head and told her what he had heard.

"I will pray for her, son," she said. "God never gives us more than we can handle."

"Thank you, Tía Martica," he said. Then, as if something had occurred to him, he added: "Do you mind if I make a private call?"

"Of course! Let me go to my room and leave you alone."

Rodolfo waited until Martica disappeared before dialing Lissy's number. When he heard her mother's voice, he asked for her.

"She's saying goodbye to her boyfriend, but let me go get her," her mother said. "Between you and me, I don't like that boy. Just don't tell her I told you that."

"I won't."

"Let me go get her!"

Lissy answered the telephone with a "hey you!" a habit she had acquired since she'd started college.

"So, how are you?" he asked.

"Exhausted," she said. "To be honest, if my workload continues at the university, I'm not going to have time for a boyfriend. Entrance to medical school is very competitive."

He didn't understand why, but her statement relieved him.

"So... what's going on?" she added.

"Why do you think something is going on?" he replied.

"You always call me when something worries you. Am I wrong?"

"No," he said. "You're right. I shouldn't bother you with my problems."

"That's not what I meant, you silly! We're friends, right? You can call me any time you want. So what's wrong?"

He proceeded to tell her about the breakup of his parents and his concerns that his mother was an alcoholic.

"That's a rushed conclusion," she answered. "Your mother may have had a few extra drinks before she called you, but that doesn't make her an alcoholic."

"It's not just that. Both my father and my sister left her. He would've never done that. There had to be a big reason for him to just walk away."

"You don't think their inability to leave Cuba is the reason?" Lissy asked.

"I don't."

"Well, you know them better than I do, but you can't worry about things you have no control over," she said. "Time helps us heal. Trust me. It does. *I* know."

"What do you mean?"

"Oh, it's nothing."

Chapter 13

"I have one more thing to tell you," he said. "The reason I called my mother was to tell her about my acceptance to the University of Miami. I start in the fall."

"Oh my God! Congratulations! I love it here, and I'm sure you will too. It is a big campus, you know? It may be a little intimidating going from a community college to a university, but I'm sure you'll adapt in no time."

"And if not, I always have you to keep me out of trouble," he said.

They laughed.

"I'm good at that, right?"

"Yes, you are."

"Before I go back to my studying, there's something I wanted to tell you," she said.

"What is it?"

"Things are getting a little more serious with my boyfriend," she said. "He has been talking about marriage lately."

"What?" he asked. "You're not considering marrying him, are you?"

"I don't know," she said.

"Lissy, you're too good for him. You are going to be a doctor one day. You have to think this through. There has to be someone better out there for you than that guy."

"Like who?"

"Listen... Let's talk about it when you finish your semester. We need to talk before you go forward with this nonsense. Do you promise you won't make any decisions until we talk?"

"Fine... I promise."

CHAPTER 14

As agreed, during the last week of the semester, Rodolfo called Lissy to set a day and time for their dinner. He was nervous to see her again after almost six months of speaking to her only over the telephone. By then, with the money from his part-time job, Rodolfo had bought a 1965 red Chevrolet Impala with over 85,000 miles on it. Having a car increased his confidence and made him more assertive. He now had conversations with Arturo about politics and was no longer afraid to participate in discussions when Martica invited friends to the house. Having a car also gave him more job options. A couple of months after he purchased it, he'd accepted a part-time job at an engineering firm paying a dollar more per hour than what he had been making. During a time when the minimum wage was $1.60 per hour, making $3.50 per hour made him feel good about himself.

His new job energized him with the idea of one day being able to bring his parents and little sister to the United States and buying them a place of their own. Not that a small bump in salary would help him get there. He understood the road ahead was difficult and long, but at least he now had the means to buy a girl a meal at a decent restaurant.

Moments after he knocked on Lissy's door, Sara greeted him with a big smile.

"Oh my God," she said giving him a hug and a kiss on the cheek. "Look at you! You're no longer the skinny teenager I met about three years ago. Looking good! But don't stand there. Come in!"

Rodolfo's slick back hairstyle complemented his square face. He wore a blue long-sleeve shirt, no tie, and dark blue pants. Before he had a chance to sit down, Lissy appeared in the living room wearing a yellow sleeveless blouse, a short beige skirt—a couple of inches above her knee— and brown heels. She wore her hair down, a thin-colorful band around her head.

"Hi!" Lissy said and gave Rodolfo a joyful kiss on the cheek, while noticing the scent of his Pierre Cardin cologne.

He looked at Lissy sideways, trying not to stare at her like a creep, right in front of her mother. He swallowed, feeling his heart accelerating, but telling himself he needed to remain cool.

"We're leaving, Mom," she said, kissing her mother on the cheek. Relief at last. That's what Rodolfo felt when Lissy said goodbye to her mother.

"But I was going to bring him some coffee," her mother replied, her eyes traveling from Lissy's face down to her shoes. "Look at you, missy, dressed with that hippie band around your head. And that skirt. Hmm…"

Rodolfo told himself not to look at Lissy again, so instead his eyes focused on his mother, anything but Lissy.

"They're in style, Mom," Lissy said with confidence. "Remember? You were my age once."

Lissy's mother shook her head. "Don't remind me. The two of you are making me old." Then turning her eyes toward Rodolfo, she added, "Please take care of my daughter."

Rodolfo smiled and nodded as he felt the blood rush to his face. Later, as he drove away, he couldn't stop looking in Lissy's direction every once in a while.

"Can you watch the traffic?" she asked, noticing his looks. "Is there something wrong with my clothes?"

"Not at all," he said. "You look beautiful."

Lissy's face reddened.

"Don't forget I have a boyfriend, mister."

Now that they were alone, he felt a burst of confidence returning.

"Boyfriends don't bother me," he said, trying to act cool.

"Look at you! Acting all grownup."

They smiled, and she gave his arm a playful push. Moments later, she reached for the dial of the radio and began searching for music. She stopped at a station that was playing *If You Don't Know Me by Now.*

"I love this song," she said.

"It's very appropriate," he replied.

"What do you mean?"

"Oh... Nothing."

She glanced at him and tilted her head, as if trying to decipher what he was thinking.

"So... where are you taking me?" she asked.

"Versailles Restaurant," he said. "One of my friends recommended it."

"My mom told me about it!" she replied, opening her eyes wide. "Jerry took her there for Valentine's Day."

"So, we'll make today our Valentine's Day," he said.

"I told you I have a boyfriend," she said.

Taking one of his hands off the steering wheel for a moment, he made believe he was playing an invisible violin. She laughed.

The restaurant, located minutes from Lissy's house, had a small crowd of people waiting to be seated, but the wait was shorter than Lissy and Rodolfo had anticipated. They sat by a tall glass-and-wood window with views of the parking lot, not romantic by any means, but more private than in the middle of the crowded restaurant.

"So why did you want to talk to me before I tell my boyfriend whether or not I'll marry him?" she asked after the waiter took their order and disappeared towards the back of the restaurant.

He took a sip from his Coca Cola and looked into her eyes.

"Because I don't want you to say yes," he said.

"Why not?"

Chapter 14

"He's not the right person for you," he replied, staring at her from across the small table.

"And who is the right person?" She too took a sip from her soda and glanced at him.

"I am," he said with assertiveness, looking into her eyes.

"But you've never considered me girlfriend material," she said. "What changed?"

"You were not the type of girlfriend I was looking for at the time," he said. "You were a nice girl. That was not what I needed then."

He lied and regretted it the moment he did, but he didn't want to belittle himself in front of her.

"Did I stop becoming nice over night?"

"It's not that," he said. "You're still nice, but I'm ready for nice..." He paused for a moment. He couldn't keep lying because he realized he would lose her. "Look, since the day we met, I knew I could always count on you. You've been my only friend and confidant. Every time my life turns upside down, you are there to help me straighten it. I won't allow someone else to take from me the best thing in my life."

She gave him a bitter smile and shook her head.

"Why are you looking at me like that?" he asked.

"You never noticed it, did you?" she asked.

"Notice what?"

"That I was in love with you since I first saw you," she said.

He gave her a perplexed look. He started to reach for her hand, but the waiter arrived with their food, so she removed her hands from the table and placed them in her lap.

"I'm sorry; I didn't know," he said, after the waiter left. "I'm very sorry. There was so much happening back then. But even if I had, that would not have changed anything."

"Why not?" she asked. "That's right. A man has needs. I wasn't able to fulfill them back then because I was a nice girl." She leaned forward, moving her head close to his. "Don't you understand I would've allowed you to be with whomever you had to, even if it broke my heart, because I loved you?"

"I... didn't know. Please give me a chance to make it right. We're made for each other. You know that."

"Rodolfo, you can't do this," she said. "It took me a long time to let you go. I accepted it and moved on."

"Just answer one question," he said. "Are you truly happy?"

She remained quiet.

"If the answer is no, you have to give me a chance to make you happy. I don't want to go through life wondering how it could've been between us. Can we give us a try?"

"What about Tony?

"Leave him," he said, looking into her eyes. "Even if things don't work out, he's not the right man for you."

"I... don't know," she said. "I need to think this through. I just need time. I think we should talk about something else."

Chapter 14

As always, she led the conversation and talked about family, the protests against the war, and the Republican National Convention that was coming to Miami, anything but them. Rodolfo mentioned his uncle had an invitation to the Republican National Convention. Not surprising. After all, Arturo was the eternal Republican, no matter what position the party took. Rodolfo went along with whatever topics Lissy wanted to discuss, but he felt compelled to save this night. This could be his last chance to make things right. He told her he had a surprise for her after the meal. Some fresh air might do them both good, he said.

After they finished their main course, they ate a creamy flan, Lissy's favorite dessert, and this one didn't disappoint. The mixture of condensed and evaporated milks, cream cheese, and eggs topped with caramel sauce, was the best invention the Cubans had ever had. That was what Lissy said, because according to her mother, it was the Cubans who placed the "f" into the flan. Rodolfo disagreed.

"The flan was invented by the Romans, and it survived the fall of the Roman Empire. The Spaniards made it sweeter by adding caramel on top, but the Cubans have nothing to do with it."

Lissy rolled her eyes. Rodolfo would have to argue that point with Lissy's mother, and good luck with that, she said.

Rodolfo tried to keep his next destination a surprise, but the moment Lissy noticed they had left the lights of downtown behind and were heading for the bridge leading to the beaches, she figured out where he was taking her. As he drove through the Miami Beach area, Rodolfo admired the majestic palm trees and the Art Deco architecture. He stopped for a brief moment near the Sahara Hotel to take a picture of Lissy in front of a statue of an Arab man and his camels. But the 1970s was a time of economic decline in Miami Beach, when mostly the elderly frequented the motels to relax and play shuffleboard. Rodolfo parked on Ocean Drive, next to the beach and across from a row of brightly lit restaurants and hotels. They removed their shoes and walked on the sand, along the edge of the water.

"It is nice here," she said, breathing in the ocean air.

The pie-shaped moon illuminated the dark waters while the waves caressed the sand. They walked for a while, leaving the busier area of the beach behind and passing by a row of hotels with direct access to the beach.

"If we keep walking, we will be back after midnight," she said.

"Do you want to sit for a while?" he asked.

"This skirt is too short," she said.

"I'll take off my shirt so you can cover your legs with it."

"What a gentleman," she observed.

"For you, Lissy, anything."

The moment she saw him shirtless, she nervously looked the other way.

"Is something wrong?" he asked.

"I'm a mess. Some things never change."

"I don't understand."

"Have you been working out?" she asked.

Chapter 14

"Oh, my muscles make you nervous?"

She took a deep breath. He handed her his shirt, and she covered her legs with it as she sat on the sand.

"I'm not saying anything else," she said with a playful smile. "Like I told you before, I have a boyfriend, and I should not be here with you."

"But the point is that you *are* here," he said, sitting very close to her. They remained in silence for a while, facing each other. Lissy looked down, but Rodolfo couldn't keep his eyes off of her. His hands then reached for her face and caressed it. "You are so pretty," he said. "If you asked for that moon you see in the sky, I'd do everything I could to bring it to you."

Evading his eyes, Lissy rubbed her thigh. He reached for her hand and held it within his, noticing it was freezing.

"Give me a chance to show you that I'm the one," he said.

"We should go," she whispered.

He came closer to her, so close he could feel her breathing and smell her flowery perfume.

"God, you're so beautiful, Lissy," he said, and his lips drifted to hers while he pulled her close. His lips met hers hungrily, a torrent of passion pouring from him, and soon he found himself on top her, her back against the sand. At first, she surrendered to him, her eyes closed, her body trembling. Then, all of a sudden, she pushed him away.

"I have a boyfriend," she said. "Please take me home."

Disappointed, he let her go.

"Break up with him, Lissy," he said.

She stood up, straightening her clothes, and returned his shirt to him.

"I'm sorry I allowed this to happen," she said.

"I'm not. Break up with him, please."

"We should've left things the way they were."

"But things can never be the same," he said.

She looked at him for a moment, then turned around and walked away briskly. He followed her, and when he caught up with her, he stayed by her side, but they both remained in silence until they made it back to his car. When he opened the door for her, she thanked him. Later, as he drove away, he glanced at her for a moment.

"Can you tell me why?" he asked.

"I don't want to get hurt," she said.

"So, your solution is marrying someone you don't love? Besides, what makes you think I would hurt you?"

"Until now, I've been invisible to you as a woman," she said. "You've talked to me about your girlfriend without regard to how that made me feel. And now, when I tell you that I'm considering marrying someone else that changes everything. That doesn't make sense. I've come to realize I have to leave my past behind. Cuba is my past, and *you* are my past. Let's stay as friends."

"I'll prove myself to you," he said, taking his eyes away from the road for a moment to glance at her. "Just give me a chance."

"Let's not complicate things," she said. "One day, you will return to Cuba, find that girl you left behind, and I'll be just a memory. My life is here in the United States."

"Who said I had plans to return?" he asked, shaking his head.

"Your mother forced you to come," she said. "You have nothing against the political system that took *everything* away from me," she said with a rapid shooting of words.

"What about me?" he asked, glancing at her for a moment before his eyes returned to the road. "They're not allowing *my* parents to leave. Don't you think this changed things for me? Do you think I give a damn about the Castro government?"

"I don't know what you think," she said. "You've never been very vocal about your position when it comes to politics, while I want nothing to do with Castro or anything that reminds me of everything I've lost."

"I want *nothing* to do with that government either, and have no interest in returning to Cuba, other than to see my family. And I don't even know if that day will come. I'm sorry I didn't say this before. I just don't like talking about my feelings."

He took a deep breath. This was not how he had imagined this evening, but giving up was not an option he was willing to consider. They remained in silence until he stopped in front of her house.

"Lissy," he said, looking at her. "I know you better than anyone else. You have a kind heart, and you care about people. I understand things were not the way they should've been. But you must understand. I was new to this country. I didn't have a car or make any money. You, on the other hand, come from a family who had a different economic status. I never thought someone like you would be interested in someone like me."

"Then why now?" she asked.

"I have a job, a car. It's not much, but I also plan to be an engineer one day. I will not make as much as a doctor, but I hope it counts for something. Look... All I know is I'm willing to fight for you if you let me, and if you think I deserve someone like you."

"This is not about how much you make," she said. "I don't think in those terms."

"Then don't marry your boyfriend, please. Could you promise me that?"

The lights of the porch in Lissy's house were on, and Rodolfo saw someone looking out through the curtains.

"When I become an engineer and get a job that is worthy of you, I will ask you to marry me. That's my promise to you."

"You can't promise that," she said. "That's two years away. A lot can happen in between."

"Nothing will change how I feel."

"But you will meet other people," she said.

"I want no one else."

Rodolfo noticed that someone had opened the front door slightly. He concluded it had to be Lissy's mother.

"I can't promise you anything," she said.

Chapter 14

"Just promise me you won't get married. That's all I ask."

"Can we stay as friends for now?" she asked.

"If that's what you want, yes. But I can't promise that I won't stop trying to change your mind."

"It will be simpler if we stayed as friends."

They kissed each other on the cheek and she told him not to accompany her to the door. However, he remained parked in front of her house until she went in and the lights of the porch were turned off. He then drove away thinking that nothing would be simple going forward. He was angry at himself for not seeing the obvious and letting her slip away. The thought of her body so close to his and her lips' sweet surrender to his kiss drove him crazy, and for the first time in his life, he decided not to let situations define his future. He was ready to fight for her.

CHAPTER 15

Rodolfo and Lissy decided not to take the summer off from school. As busy as they were with their schedules, he had to find a less disruptive method than a telephone call to convey to her how he felt about her. That's when he thought about sending her letters—like those his grandfather used to send to his grandmother in Cuba when they were secretly dating.

Knowing how to romance a woman through letters was not in his arsenal of skills. He had to learn by visiting the library and reading books on the subject. In his first letter to her, he wrote:

Dear Lissy,

You will find this approach to attempt to conquer your heart somewhat unorthodox for modern times, but through these letters, I hope to convey what I can't by other means.

I admit that when I met you I was lost. I was trying to find myself in a new country that I didn't understand, and you brightened my path with a smile that cannot be replicated by the most talented of painters. You are my moon, my stars, and my sun, all at the same time.

Sometimes, it takes certain events in life to guide us towards the obvious. In my case, the moment you said you were considering marrying someone else, it was as if lightning had traveled through my body. I realized then that I couldn't let you fade out of my life, that you didn't belong in the arms of another, but in mine. My arms are anxious to embrace you, and my hand ready to hold yours until the last day of my life.

I will not stop writing to you until your heart opens to let me in. So I make this promise. Every two weeks, you will receive a letter from me until you say yes.

Every night, when I look at the sky, I will imagine both of us on the sand, my lips lost in yours, your light guiding me home.

I love you, Lissy.

Yours always,

Rodolfo.

Every two weeks after writing the first letter, he wrote another, and then another. Each more intense than the next, as he continued to read at the local library love letters written by other men. He didn't copy those he found in his research, but through them, he learned how to uncover his deepest feelings and bring them to paper. Once he finished writing his eighth letter, he wondered if he was wasting his time. She had not yet responded to any of them, even though in the last one, he had asked her to marry him after his graduation.

At last, on the ninth week, his aunt told him that a letter had arrived for him. Martica wasn't sure who had sent it because the return address had been left blank.

Rodolfo took the envelope and went to his bedroom. When he extracted the carefully-folded handwritten letter, he took a deep breath as he recognized Lissy's handwriting. He sat on the end of his bed and began to read.

Dear Rodolfo,

I feel awful that I haven't acknowledged any of your letters. I have read and kept each one of them. They've allowed me to discover a part of you I never knew existed, and I'm impressed and touched by your sensitivity.

Over the past four months, the memories of the night at the beach have provoked feelings in me I had not experienced before, which led me to conclude that it wasn't fair to continue my relationship with Tony. I now realize he can't unearth the feelings that pour out of me when I'm with you. This doesn't mean I'm ready to let my guard down, not yet.

Since the day I met you, you were all I could think about, and back then it took me a while to arrive at the conclusion that no matter how hard I tried, you only looked at me as a friend.

When you later told me you had a girlfriend, a pretty, care-free blond who didn't share our background or our values, I was hurt. I realized I couldn't compete with her because I couldn't give myself to you in body like she did. I was jealous. Jealousy is like a snake that devours us in a slow and painful manner. My response was to do what you did, to find someone who was diametrically opposed to the man I loved.

I tried to convince myself he was the right person for me, and for a while I believed it. That is, until that night at the beach. I was so afraid to lose myself when you had me in your arms. It still scares me, because in many ways, I'm still the naïve teenager who offered to help you when you first came to class. Unlike your girlfriend and whoever else you've been with, no one has yet robbed me of my innocence.

My mother has been indoctrinating me for years to wait until marriage before giving my body to someone, and to this date, I'm embarrassed to admit that I continue to wait. Just know that in soul, I've always been yours.

Please don't laugh. I'm sure there are few women out there like me, and chances are that many of them are Cuban.

I hope you keep my secret, like I've kept so many secrets you've shared with me. If it's true you want to marry after your graduation—as you said in your last letter—because only then, you'll be able to provide for me, I'll wait. But realize that until then, we should limit our interactions outside of our homes.

Chapter 15

I understand you have needs that I can't fulfill, at least not yet, so if you must have other women, I'll understand, but I prefer not to know.

The moment we tell our families how we feel about each other, life will get more complicated. I know my mother. Get ready for what's coming.

If all the feelings you've shared with me in your letters are true, come this weekend to my house and speak to my mother—and to my stepfather, of course. Despite our differences, he has been there for me all these years and deserves my respect.

I never thought I would say these words. I love you. I'll see you soon.

Yours,

Lissy.

Rodolfo sat at the edge of the bed with a wide smile on his face. He couldn't believe it, nor control the tear that at that moment rolled down his face. What would his father say if he learned that the letter from a woman had brought tears to his eyes? What would Arturo say? The thought of having a future with Lissy made him feel whole. It was the first time he felt that way after leaving Cuba.

Gentle knocks on his door distracted him.

"Is everything okay?" Martica asked from the other side of the door.

"Yes, Tía Martica," he said, wiping his face. "You can come in."

Chapter 15

She entered the room wearing an apron over her blue dress.

"Well?" she asked. "Who wrote to you?"

"Lissy," he said without thinking.

"What about? Is she okay?"

"I asked her to marry me, and she said yes!" he said with a triumphant smile.

"But wait a minute," she said. "I thought she was dating some other man. I don't understand."

He smiled and placed his arm around Martica.

"It's complicated, Tía Martica."

"Oh my God!" she said, giving him a hug. "I can't believe it. I knew it! From the moment I saw that girl, I told Arturo that she was perfect for you. I knew it! I'm so happy for you!"

They embraced, and then she ran out of the bedroom to tell Arturo the news.

CHAPTER 16

Rodolfo was outside the library, waiting for Lissy to finish her Organic Chemistry class, when he noticed a pretty blond approaching him and looking at him with a familiar smile. She dressed in a flouncy yellow dress and walked with a feminine poise.

"Oh my God!" she said in Spanish. "It *is* you! I almost didn't recognize you. You're so grown up and handsome."

She gave him a hug, as if she knew him.

"I'm sorry; do I know you?" he asked, shrinking his eyebrows and tilting his head.

"Don't tell me you already forgot your visit to my apartment in Costa del Sol," she said, raising her forehead.

"Aida?" he asked.

"You do remember me!" she said with joy, pinching his cheek.

"Yes, how can I forget!" he said, shaking his head. His memories of that day brought a smile to his face for a moment, but then he shook off his thoughts. "So... what are you up to these days? Are you a student?"

Chapter 16

"I just graduated with a Psychology degree, but I came to meet a friend," she said. "I'll be going back to Spain in a couple of days... Hey! I have an idea. Why don't we start where we left off, for old times' sake?"

"Thank you for the offer, but I can't," he said.

She placed her hand on his elbow. "It'll be fun. Don't be so boring."

"I'm sorry, but I'm engaged," he said.

"I'm not the jealous type," she said, with a flirtatious smile.

He shook his head. "You haven't changed," he said.

"I'm done with my class!" Rodolfo heard someone say. Recognizing Lissy's voice, he nervously turned around.

"Hi, Lissy," he said, kissing her on the cheek. "Well...ready to go?"

"Aren't you going to introduce me to your friend?" Lissy asked, glancing at Aida up and down.

"Yes, of course," Rodolfo replied. "Lissy, this is Aida."

Aida kissed Lissy on the cheek.

"It's a pleasure to meet you, Lissy," Aida said, checking out her competition. "You're very pretty." Then, turning to Rodolfo, she added: "You *do* have good taste in women."

"And how did the two of you meet?" Lissy asked.

"Didn't he tell you?" Aida replied.

Lissy stared at Rodolfo.

"No, he hasn't."

Chapter 16

"It was a long time ago, so don't worry. It was a night of fun, and that was it. Anyhow, I'll leave the two of you alone. It was great to see you, Rodolfo. Too bad you're busy. It would've been nice to catch up."

Aida gave Rodolfo a good-bye hug and a soft kiss on his cheek, and then turned to Lissy and placed her cheek against hers.

"Until we meet again," Aida said, walking away and leaving Lissy and Rodolfo facing each other. Lissy stared at him and crossed her arms.

"Can you tell me what's going on?" she asked.

"I met her when I was in Spain," he said.

"Why didn't you say anything about her?" Lissy said.

Rodolfo rubbed his face. "Can we talk in the car?"

"I'm just curious," she said, trying to hide her anger.

"Fine," he said, taking a deep breath. "I was at the beach with my family. We met. One thing led to another, and she invited me to her apartment. That's all."

Lissy waited for some students to pass by before she asked the next question.

"Did you...?"

"Lissy, don't go there."

"It's just a question."

"Yes," he said. "She was my first."

She raised her chin slightly, bringing her eyebrows together. Rodolfo noticed her disappointment.

"Let's go," she said with a sigh and a gloomy expression. "It's getting late."

She turned around and began to walk with quick steps.

"Did I do something wrong?" he asked, trying to catch up with her.

She didn't respond. Instead, she walked faster towards the parking lot and waited for him next to his car. He opened her door first and let her in. When they were both inside, he turned on the ignition and glanced at her.

"I would never want to hurt you, Lissy. You are the love of my life. You must know that."

He could tell she was on the verge of tears.

"Please say something," he said, reaching for her hand.

She turned her head away from him, towards her window. After a moment of quiet reflection, she focused her gaze on the windshield.

"I feel useless," she said with a slight shrug of her shoulders. "That's all."

"Why?" he asked, caressing her chin with his fingers.

But she couldn't look at him and instead glanced at the floor mat as she responded.

"I was raised in a conservative way, so I feel inadequate. I..." She paused and lifted her head. Her eyes then met his. "I wish I could be the woman you need now, without this stupid guilt that comes over me every time I think about us being together before we get married."

"I'm fine with your decision," he said. "Don't worry."

Chapter 16

"There are other ways I could please you without—"

"Oh, my beautiful Lissy," he said, placing his arm around her and kissing her on the lips. She began to weep. "Don't cry, my princess," he said. "You don't have to do anything that makes you feel uncomfortable. We'll make up for all the lost time after we get married."

"You're so kind," she said, giving him a hug. They kissed again passionately until he realized he should stop.

"I'm sorry," he said, leaning back against his seat and leaving her anxious for his kisses. "This is not helping."

She started to giggle like a teenage girl when she noticed what had made him stop.

"I didn't mean to get you *so* happy," she said. "I'm sorry."

He shook his head. "You're enjoying this, aren't you?"

She responded with a smile, and he shook his head and started to back out from the parking lot. Meanwhile, she could not stop giggling about his reaction to their kisses.

They had been dating for a year, and their love for each other emanated from them like a ray of sunlight. When they walked, they held hands and looked at each other as if no one else existed. Everyone noticed. Even Arturo, who at first had opposed the marriage, began to treat Lissy like a member of the family.

As Lissy had anticipated, her mother tried to get control of the preparations for the wedding while the young couple remained firm on their decision to have something simple with only the immediate family and selected friends.

During the past year, Rodolfo had written to his mother several times to tell her about Lissy and their wedding plans, and had included pictures with the letters he sent. After the announcement, his mother seemed more cheerful, but then, as before, her letters turned gloomy.

"I can't wait for you to come home, son," his mother would tell him in every letter.

And as time passed, the meaning of the word "home" became less clear to him.

CHAPTER 17

"Arturo, hurry up!" Martica shouted from the living room. "Your daughter is almost here!"

Rodolfo, Lissy, and her parents sat in the living room, all elegantly dressed, conversing with Martica. She wore a simple pearl necklace and a lilac dress she had made for the occasion. Clara had helped her decorate the house with a big sign above the sofa with white letters against a blue background reading "Congratulations graduates!" Two small teddy bears wearing caps and gowns sat on the coffee table, and balloons scattered around completed the festive appearance of the house. After a while, Martica excused herself and took two of the four empty glasses from the coffee table. Rodolfo picked up the other two and followed her into the kitchen.

"Tía Martica," Rodolfo said. "Lissy, her family, and I need to go now because the graduates have to get to the ceremony before everyone else. Take your time."

"I don't know why your uncle is taking so long," she whispered. "He has changed his shirt I don't know how many times. I think he's nervous."

"Why?" Rodolfo asked.

"And you need to ask me?" Martica said in a low tone of voice, placing her hands on her hips. "Sweetheart, do you realize how important this day is for him?" Her eyes filled with tears as she looked at her nephew with admiration. "You're a good man, Rodolfo, and God has to reward you. What you have done for your uncle can't be repaid with any sum of money. We understand that our son can't come back to us, but when God brought you into our lives, he gave us a piece of what we had lost."

He placed his hand on her shoulder.

"You have been the parents I left behind, Tía Martica," Rodolfo said. "I'm the one who needs to thank you."

He kissed her on the cheek and hugged her. "I'll see you at the graduation!" he said.

Martica wiped her face. "Let me go find him," she said. "I'll see you later."

Moments later, Rodolfo, Lissy, and her family walked out of the house at the same time that Clara, her baby, and her husband were arriving. They greeted each other with hugs and kisses.

"I have to run!" Rodolfo said. "Lissy and I will be late for graduation. See you soon!"

***

It was May 19, 1974, and the Miami Beach Convention Center was packed with families and University of Miami graduates dressed in black.

Sitting in a sea of caps and gowns, Rodolfo anxiously looked for Lissy among the students, and when he couldn't find her, he stood up briefly, and his eyes searched the perimeter. Suddenly, from a few rows away, she began to wave at him. He waved back, a happy smile adorning his expression. Moments later, he began to look for his family in the bleachers, but there were so many people.

The sound of the graduation ceremony music—as the students finished taking their seats—the cheering, and the happiness that enveloped the place made him think about his parents. He imagined them, waving at him from the bleachers, his mother dressed in an elegant blue dress and his father wearing a handsome white *guayabera* with long sleeves. His eyes filled with emotion, forcing him to look down and wipe a tear that was about to roll down his face.

Four years of hard work had led to this day, and now his life would change in unimaginable ways. He was leaving behind the little *cubanito* who hardly spoke English to replace him with an engineer soon to become an American citizen. Rodolfo and Lissy spoke about finding a new place of their own to call home, but Martica insisted he and Lissy live with them for at least a couple of years until they saved enough money for a house. She said it would give them a more solid start in their journey as husband and wife. Rodolfo had another reason to celebrate. The draft had ended, so he wouldn't have to leave Lissy behind to go to Vietnam.

Chapter 17

Life was smiling at Rodolfo, and he couldn't be happier. However, other not so pleasant surprises awaited along his path.

A few minutes after the keynote speaker concluded his remarks, students began to head towards the stage to receive their diplomas. As the announcer called their names one by one, the students walked across the platform, cheered by the crowd, while their future waited on the other side.

At the conclusion of the beautiful ceremony, families gathered outside to wait for their graduates. It took a while for Rodolfo to connect with Lissy and her family. So he stood in the middle of the crowd, searching for a familiar face and looking like an abandoned puppy. After he found them, the obligatory hugs, congratulations, and pictures followed. Still no sign of Rodolfo's family. Rodolfo and Lissy then began to search for them until little by little the families began to leave.

At last, he saw Clara holding her baby in her arms, while her husband stood by her side. He called their names, and the moment Clara heard him, she repositioned her baby on one arm and waved at Rodolfo. As she and her family began to walk toward him, Rodolfo realized that Arturo and Martica were not with them.

Clara kissed and hugged Rodolfo and Lissy, but the way she looked at him led him to conclude that something was wrong.

"Where are your parents?" he asked.

"I'll explain later," she said. "Let's take some pictures first."

Rodolfo didn't want to contradict her, but he was worried. Later, after they finished taking pictures, he excused himself and took Clara aside.

"Is everything okay?" he asked.

She shook her head.

"Dad had to be rushed to the hospital," she said. "He was having chest pain. This day was too emotional for him."

"But I don't understand," Rodolfo said. "I thought this is what he wanted."

"He did. I think the memories of my brother..."

Clara started to weep, and Rodolfo embraced her. When Lissy and her family noticed, they joined them and asked what was going on.

"What are we waiting for?" Lissy asked after she heard the news. "Let's go to the hospital! He needs us there with him."

Rodolfo glanced at her, held her hand, and nodded.

CHAPTER 18

Despite the nurses' insistence that only one person at a time could visit Arturo, the entire family ended up trickling into his room. By then, Arturo had already undergone a series of tests and was feeling better than he did when he arrived at the hospital. Instead of remaining quiet, like he usually did, he talked with the men about politics, while the women discussed the upcoming wedding.

Upon entering Arturo's room, the head nurse raised her eyebrows when she noticed the multiple conversations in progress at the time. "Sorry," she said. "Only one of you can stay here. The rest, please wait outside in the waiting area."

Martica pleaded with the nurse, but in the end only one person could remain in the room.

"Rodolfo, can you stay?" Arturo said as everyone except Martica, headed for the door after saying goodbye to him. Then, turning to his wife, he added: "Martica, Rodolfo will find you when we are done."

Martica nodded. "Of course, *mi amor.* I'll be outside. Rodolfo, if he needs anything, please come get me."

Chapter 18

After the family left the two men alone, Arturo remained silent for a while. Rodolfo sat on a chair next to his uncle, looking around the room and shaking his leg.

"Do you need anything, Arturo?" Rodolfo asked. "Water, juice, anything?"

"You don't need to call me Arturo anymore. Tío or Tío Arturo is fine."

Rodolfo nodded while Arturo shook his head and smiled with a look of admiration in his eyes.

"Coñó!" Arturo said. It was the first time Rodolfo had heard his uncle curse, but in this case, the word had not been said in anger but in amazement. "I can't believe it! You finally did it! At last we have an engineer in the family, and after you marry Lissy, we'll have a doctor too."

Rodolfo smiled.

"I'm proud of you, son," Arturo said.

"Thank you, Tío, but now that your wishes came true, you have to start taking care of yourself."

"I don't know what happened." Arturo replied, bringing his eyebrows together and musing over what had occurred. "I was in your room at the time, looking at some of the pictures and... everything started spinning around me. Luckily, the bed is in the middle of the room now, and I was able to hold on to it before I hit the floor."

"You work too much, Tío," Rodolfo said.

"I think Martica is exaggerating. This is probably nothing. I'm just getting old."

"The doctors need to confirm there's nothing else going on. You already had a minor heart attack."

Arturo waved his hand dismissively. "Can you do me a favor?" he asked, and without waiting for his nephew to reply, he added. "You see that plastic bag on that chair? My wallet is inside. Bring it to me."

Rodolfo obeyed. Arturo unfolded his wallet, extracted a picture, and handed it to Rodolfo.

"This was my son, Fernandito," he said.

Rodolfo examined it for a while. He had seen other pictures of his cousin in his room, but on this one, he looked more like Rodolfo than in the others.

"It's true what Clara said," Rodolfo said. "We look like brothers."

Rodolfo returned the picture to his uncle.

"When I took my son out of Cuba," Arturo said while contemplating the picture, "he was fifteen. All I ever wanted was to keep him and my family safe. That's all!" Arturo's voice cracked as he said this, and his eyes filled with tears. Arturo pounded the bed with his closed fists. "Goddammit, my son was my life!" He paused and took a deep breath. "Part of me wonders what would've happened if we'd stayed in Cuba. All I know is that I failed him, and I failed Martica because when she needed me the most, when my son's body was lying in a funeral home, she had to handle everything because *I*, the tough man, the man who at one point in his life thought he was invincible, fell apart."

Arturo started to weep.

Chapter 18

"I failed them—"

When overcome with emotion, Arturo could not finish his phrase. Rodolfo rose from his chair, patted him on the shoulder, and handed him a cup of water and a tissue.

"Come on, Tío," Rodolfo said. "Talking about this is not good for you."

Arturo took a sip of water and took a deep breath. "I can't imagine how it must have been for Martica," Arturo continued as he wiped his face with the tissue. "I remember my mother telling me for as long as she lived that there was no greater love than the love of a mother. Yet, when I lost my son, when he left me, he took my soul with him. He took my ability to feel and to love and to care about anything or anyone. Imagine how Martica, that angel of a woman, the woman who carried him inside her for nine months, who would have given her life for his, imagine how she must have felt. But I couldn't help her. That's why since then, I'd lock myself in the Cuba Room, like Clarita calls it, with my son's pictures, with my memories of Cuba. This way, I could relive that fucking pain over and over again, because only then I could feel something."

Rodolfo's emotions gathered in the corner of his eyes. He sat on the chair next to his uncle's bed and patted his arm.

"How did he die? Rodolfo asked.

"He had just started college. He went out with a friend to get some lunch," Arturo said wiping a tear. "They never saw the truck approaching. He died instantly..."

He paused for a moment and glanced at the picture of his son again.

"All I ever wanted was to keep him safe, but by bringing him here, I killed him." Arturo said.

"You can't think this way, Tío Arturo," Rodolfo said, moving his chair closer to his uncle's bed. "My grandmother always said that we all came to this world with our *destino* prewritten. Also, I'm not very religious because in Cuba people can't openly practice religion, but Clara and Tía Martica believe that my cousin is in Heaven and that he's watching us from above. What if they're right?"

"I don't know what to think," Arturo said. "I've been so angry with God for taking him away. It's not fair, you know? There are so many people who commit crimes, from selling drugs to killing people. And I keep asking myself, why did God take away a good boy that was just starting college, a kind boy who was always helping others, someone who could have done so much good? It makes no fucking sense. I miss him *so* much, and you remind me of him. You have the same glow in your eyes he did."

Arturo paused for a moment and smiled as he recalled the past. "You know? When he was growing up, I would take him to the park to play catch," Arturo said. "He loved it! He also played dominos with me, not because he cared about it, but to make me happy."

Rodolfo smiled and nodded.

"When I was growing up, my dad and I went to the Santos Suárez Park to play catch too. Good times."

Chapter 18

"We should do that when I get out of the hospital," Arturo suggested.

"Make sure you clear that with your doctor and Dr. Martica first."

They both laughed.

Rodolfo stayed with his uncle for a while longer.

"Rodolfo, you better go get Martica," Arturo said. "She must be getting worried. It was good talking to you. Thank you for listening."

"Whenever you want to talk, I'm here for you," Rodolfo said and embraced his uncle before exiting the room.

Later, when the doctor arrived, Martica had already relieved Rodolfo. It was then she learned that Arturo's episode resulted from his reluctance to take his blood pressure medication.

"I can't emphasize how important it is for you to keep your blood pressure under control," the doctor told Arturo. "If you don't want to have a stroke, take your medication."

"I'll stay on top of it for him, Doctor," Martica said. "Our nephew is getting married soon, and my husband is the best man. He needs to be in good shape for the wedding and for his grandchildren. Besides, I don't know what I would do if I lost him."

Arturo reached for his wife's hand and held it.

"You have a good wife," the doctor said. "Listen to her."

"A good wife indeed, Doctor," Arturo said.

Arturo was discharged that evening, and over the next few weeks, the preparations for his

Chapter 18

nephews' wedding became the focal point of family life.

CHAPTER 19

After graduation, the firm where Rodolfo worked gave him a full time job as an entry level engineer, and his take home wages doubled. Despite the higher income, he remained conservative in his spending but insisted in repaying his uncle the money he had contributed toward his education. Rodolfo also had to consider the rampant inflation, which meant that a portion of his take-home pay was consumed by the higher prices of consumer goods. At least, he didn't need to worry about Lissy's education, as it was covered mostly by scholarships, with Jerry paying any remaining costs. Jerry also paid for most of the wedding expenses. He told Lissy that would be his gift to her.

Lissy and Rodolfo decided to marry in the summer, so their honeymoon would not interfere with Lissy's first semester at medical school.

Two months after graduation, Rodolfo found himself standing in front of the altar at St. John Bosco Catholic Church on Flagler Avenue, Arturo, his best man, by his side as Rodolfo waited for Lissy to make her entrance into the church.

Although they had tried to keep the wedding as small as possible, seventy-five guests attended the ceremony. Among them were Cuban exiles, most in their forties and fifties who had left their homes as adults to start a new life in the United States; their children, who each day found themselves increasingly knitted into the fabric of the North American society; and their friends, many young, outgoing, and curious about the Cubans and their culture.

Rodolfo never looked happier than when his bride appeared, her long black hair in thick curls bouncing against her white lace dress, her black eyes adorned by long eyelashes and a thin brown line beneath them. When he saw her, his smile became a sun, and when their gazes locked, their love permeated through every corner of the church, enveloping the guests. Husbands and wives among the crowd held hands and, for a brief moment, they glanced at each other before returning their eyes to the young couple about to start their journey.

Even Arturo found himself caught in the magic that enveloped the church, especially after the bride and groom held hands. When he saw his nephew and Lissy next to each other, exchanging nervous glances as the priest began to read the scriptures, his eyes glistened. Arturo then looked at Martica, who smiled while her eyes filled with happy tears.

After the reading of the scriptures and the promises between the groom and bride, the priest declared Rodolfo and Lissy husband and wife. Rodolfo turned to his bride, noticing the shine in her eyes, and they kissed, a kiss filled with love that made the crowd rise from their seats and cheer.

A reception followed at a banquet hall; nothing extravagant, but reflective of the simplicity the couple shared. And when the moment came for the father-daughter dance and the mother-son dance, Jerry danced with Lissy and Martica with Rodolfo, while Lissy thought about her dead father and Rodolfo about the parents he had left behind.

After the reception, the couple spent two nights at the Biltmore Hotel, a gift from Martica that she had paid for with the proceeds from her sewing jobs, despite her husband's complaints that she was throwing money away. After a heated argument, she stood up from her rocking chair, approached Arturo, and placed his hand in hers. "Let me have the son I lost for one day; let me give Rodolfo what I would have given our son," Martica said, her eyes full of emotion. Arturo then realized that this was a fight he would not win.

***

Once the reception clerk handed the keys to Rodolfo, he and Lissy exchanged smiles and flirtatious glances.

"I am so happy," she said on their way to the room.

"Me too. I love you, my beautiful Lissy."

Chapter 19

Later, when they entered the room and found themselves alone, he held her close and kissed her on her lips. Their passion for each other then poured from them in the form of desperate, unrestrained kisses and touching until now, forbidden. When he reached for the zipper in the back of her dress, she trembled.

"Are you afraid?" he asked, kissing her on her cheeks softly.

"It's my first time...I'm embarrassed," she whispered.

He smiled and caressed her face.

"I am so in love with you," he said. "Let me make it easier. Let's get on the bed, and you can undress under the sheets. Will that help?"

Her timid shrug conveyed her acceptance. Once they were both in bed, he fully undressed, and she still clothed, he reached for her zipper, unclasped her bra, and slipped her dress down to her torso.

"Now I will need a little help to take it off," he said, giggling.

"Oh my God, you must think that this is the worst wedding night ever."

"Not really. It is exactly how I imagined it."

They kissed again in a playful manner, and she lifted her body to allow him to remove her dress. Once all items of clothing were off, he touched her in places no one had ever touched, feeling her with desire but also provoking her laughter.

"What now?" he asked.

"Nervous laugh," she said. She took a deep breath and reduced her laughter down to a giggle.

Chapter 19

"I'll be good," she said. "I promise."

After a while of playful touching and kissing, he lay on top of her and they consummated their marriage with passion and longing for each other. Despite the pain she felt when he pierced her virginity, the pleasure of his touch, the exhilaration provoked by his warm lips on her skin, made her scream in ecstasy.

The next morning, they woke up in each other's arms, happy to have found each other, excited about the journey ahead.

CHAPTER 20

During the presidency of Richard Nixon, an energy crisis developed, resulting in the rationing of fuel and long lines at the pumps. Rampant inflation led to wage and price controls, and a general state of chaos to which Rodolfo's family was not immune. To help Arturo with expenses, he and Lissy agreed to live with them, which also allowed the couple to save money while Lissy attended medical school.

On July 25, 1974, Arturo and his family watched President Nixon's speech about the state of the economy. Nixon blamed the economic decline to a decrease in the world's grain production, resulting from bad weather; the quadrupling of oil prices by oil-producing nations; and an economic boom in industrialized nations. By then, although the Vietnam War continued, Nixon had withdrawn all United States forces from that country, following the signing of the Paris Peace Accords in 1973.

After Nixon's speech, Arturo didn't waste any time in his assessment of the situation.

Chapter 20

"It's the Arabs," he said. "Why would they quadruple prices? Don't they have enough wealth?"

"It's all about supply and demand, Tío," Rodolfo explained.

Arturo waved his hand in dismissal.

"You don't know what you're talking about; you were taught by leftists," Arturo said. "Supply and demand... Don't give me that nonsense. Like I said, it's the Arabs!"

"Well," Rodolfo replied, "I agree that OPEC's embargo against the United States is not helping things."

"Do you think that just because you've attended a university a little longer than me, that makes me stupid?"

"I would never say that, Tío," Rodolfo said with a smile, patting him on the back.

The telephone rang, and the relief on Martica's face was instant as she walked to the kitchen to answer. She was happy when she heard her daughter's voice.

"I'm glad you called, Clarita," Martica said. "I'm tired of all the politics."

"Men and their politics," Clara replied. "I have some news of my own that will take Dad's mind away from the politics, at least for a while."

"Is everything okay?"

"Yes, Mom. The timing is not great, but we'll manage."

"What's going on?"

"I'm pregnant!"

"Oh no!" Martica said. "As rough as things are now with the economy—"

"You're not happy?" Clara asked as if she had not anticipated her mother's reaction.

"Of course, I am, my love," said Martica. "I will always support you, no matter what. I just hear your dad and the president talk about the situation, and I'm worried."

"Don't worry, Mom," she said. "I'm a nurse manager. My husband also makes good money. Besides, I have you to help me with the baby. Who better than you? This situation can't last forever."

"I'm sorry about my reaction," Martica said. "The inflation, the war, and the protests all over the country... all this scares me, but I'll try to be positive. Congratulations to you and your husband. I'm sure everything will be fine."

Yet the country had not seen the end of the problems. On August 8, 1974, Arturo and his family watched Richard Nixon's resignation speech. It lasted about sixteen minutes, and during its course, the president only admitted to mistakes in his handling of the Watergate investigations. Arturo kept shaking his head and pressing his lips throughout the short speech. When it ended, Arturo arose abruptly.

"This is a witch-hunt!" he yelled and left the room.

Arturo's outrage did not end there.

After Vice President Gerald R. Ford took the oath of office following Nixon's resignation, he declared, "My fellow Americans, our long national nightmare is over."

His statement divided the country and many families like Arturo's. While Arturo supported Nixon, Clara agreed with Ford's declaration. When in September 1974, Ford pardoned Nixon for any crimes he may have committed while in office, the heated arguments between Clara and her father about the subject ended.

But another event would stir Arturo's emotions to the core: the communists' takeover of Saigon in April 1975. On one hand, he was happy that the horrors of the war no longer plagued the people of Vietnam, but he feared what would happen to the country under communist rule. He told Rodolfo in private that he felt as if he were reliving Castro's takeover of Cuba all over again. Arturo's anger during his conversation with Rodolfo raised concerns in the family about whether his blood pressure medication was working properly.

At Lissy's insistence, Arturo, accompanied by Martica, visited his doctor. His blood pressure was so high the doctor toyed with the idea of sending Arturo to the emergency room. When Martica explained that his fear of doctors may have affected his reading, the doctor increased his medication and sent him home.

While life in the United States faced a number of challenges, Cuba was kept on life support with the aid of the Soviet Union. Many of the few products the Cuban people could purchase using their ration cards came from that country. The Soviet presence was also felt in the Santos Suárez neighborhood, where a Russian woman had moved with her Cuban husband. That was what Ana had told Rodolfo in one of her letters.

Chapter 20

Rodolfo wrote to his mother at least once a month while her letters came three or four times a year... at least for a while.

CHAPTER 21

During the first few years of marriage, Rodolfo and Lissy didn't spend much time together due to their hectic schedules. While Lissy attended medical school, Rodolfo prepared to become a Professional Engineer (PE), a designation with experience requirements and intensive competency exams. On weekends, as their studies allowed, they went to the movies or to inexpensive cafes on Calle Ocho. They enjoyed spending time with their families. The men played dominoes at Arturo's house and talked about politics, while the women went to Midway Mall on West Flagler Street to help Clara shop for clothes for her children or to walk around and enjoy each other's company. Rodolfo joined the ladies sometimes, triggering the teasing from the other men in the family who said that Lissy had Rodolfo under her thumb. The women in the family enjoyed Rodolfo's chivalry. He opened the door for them, carried their heavy packages, and held Lissy's hand when they walked in the mall.

"They're so in love," Martica would say, crossing her arms over her chest. She kept asking them when the babies were coming, and the couple would tell her not to worry. "In due time, Tía; don't worry," Rodolfo replied. They had to pave a solid financial future first. Seeing the years pass by, Martica did worry. She wanted to see Rodolfo's children grow up and run around the house, like Clara's children did when they visited. She wanted to be a grandmother to his children.

The main source of discord among the family members was politics. Clara and her husband were democrats. They had kept it a secret from Arturo for fear he would have a heart attack if he learned the truth, but as the time to vote came near in 1976, Arturo overheard Clara tell Rodolfo that she was voting for Jimmy Carter.

"My own flesh and blood voting for a democrat?" Arturo said. "I left my home so you could live in a free country. And this is how you repay me? By voting for someone who's on the side of the socialists?"

Martica took the children to the back of the house and begged Arturo to stop, but his face tightened in anger and turned red.

"But Dad," Clara explained, "he's a conservative democrat who believes in small government."

"He believes in income redistribution, just like the socialists," Arturo said, pointing at her with his index finger.

"Dad, have you read about his positions? He wants people on welfare to be trained so they can get off government assistance."

Rodolfo, glad Lissy wasn't there to witness the argument, stood several steps behind Arturo and waved his hands from side to side, begging his cousin to stop. She did, after noticing the reddening on her father's face and the sweat that had gathered on his forehead. That year, Clara voted for Jimmy Carter but told her father she had voted for Ford. She never touched the subject again while at her father's house. Rodolfo listened to his uncle and kept his political views to himself, while concentrating on his future. As far as he was concerned, family came first, and each person had the freedom to think as they wished.

As time passed, Rodolfo continued to exchange letters with his mother, but with less frequency than before. There wasn't much to say, except for those rare occasions when he had something important to tell her, like when he and Lissy purchased their three-bedroom house, and later, when he was upgrading his new home. The passage of time erased his hope of returning home one day to see his parents... that is, until 1979.

By then, Rodolfo was almost twenty-seven years old and worked at the same engineering firm that had hired him when he was attending the University of Miami. He had received his Professional Engineer license, which came with a good salary increase. After finishing medical school, Lissy had started her residency at Jackson Memorial Hospital. When Lissy heard the news, she was in the break room eating a guava pastry, and washing it down with a *malta*—a refreshing malt beverage. At first, she thought she was imagining things, but after confirming what she thought she'd heard with a coworker, she rushed to the telephone to call her husband at work.

"Rodolfo, did you hear the news!" Lissy asked.

"What news?

"Exiles can go back to Cuba to visit their relatives! Cuba lifted the travel restrictions," she replied, unable to contain her happiness.

"What?"

"It was just announced! You can finally visit your parents."

Rodolfo remained in silence for a moment.

"Is Clara putting you up to this? Is this a joke?"

"It's not. I wouldn't do that to you. You need to hurry! Get your papers in order and book a flight before Castro changes his mind."

"Okay. Let me look into it."

Once Rodolfo confirmed the news, he asked Lissy if she wanted to go with him. She said she had no interest in going back, but she would only to please him. They talked about it. Rodolfo realized that asking Lissy to use her limited time off to go to Cuba was not fair to her. He might as well have asked her to relive her father's assassination all over again. Also, she wasn't interested in spending a dollar to benefit the government that had killed her father. To complicate things, the couple had already paid for a trip to Europe to take place during Lissy's vacation later that year, a much better use of her time off. So Rodolfo had no option but to go alone. As part of his planning, he needed to ready himself mentally for the return and purchase food and clothes to take to his family.

When Martica heard that Rodolfo was planning on visiting his parents, she told her husband she wanted to accompany him. Like Lissy, Arturo had no interest in going back, but Martica was more sentimental about the place where her children were born. She stood in front of her husband, waiting for his response. He stopped reading the newspaper, folded it, and placed it on the end table.

"This is a journey he needs to make alone, Martica," Arturo said with a caring gaze, as if he knew how she would react.

Her eyes filled with tears.

"I just don't want to lose him. That's all."

Arturo didn't say anything. He got off the couch, walked towards her, and gave her a warm embrace.

He didn't seem to care about the trip to Cuba until two days before Rodolfo was scheduled to leave, when he showed up at Rodolfo's house.

"Listen," Arturo said, handing Rodolfo the bag. "I'm lending you my camera so you can take a few pictures of the family, but bring it back, okay?"

"I will," Rodolfo replied.

"Inside the bag, there is an envelope with a letter for my sister and some money. Bring me a picture of her. Don't forget."

Rodolfo agreed.

The sudden lifting of travel restriction to Cuba impacted not only Rodolfo, but thousands of families as well, and before long, about 100,000 people would travel to the island to see their relatives after years of separation.

Cuba's infrastructure was not ready for such an influx, nor was it prepared to handle the unintended consequences that this opening would have on those who had stayed behind. Returning exiles were perceived as wealthy to ordinary Cubans, who felt that in their country, time had stood still. Exiles spoke about the amazing life they had lived in the United States, describing the supermarkets—packed with food—where no ration card was needed to make a purchase. So those who often had as a meal water with sugar and a piece of bread sprinkled with oil and salt began to idolize life in the United States.

Exiles who left Cuba as traitors were received by the people with open arms and greeted by relatives and neighbors with sumptuous meals of pork, beans, rice, and vegetables, purchased from the farmers in black market transactions; meals that those who stayed behind could only afford with the money brought by their relatives.

To evade the number-of-pounds controls, upon entry to the island exiles would travel to Cuba wearing multiple pairs of underwear, dresses, and pants, or with clothes stuffed inside their bras or underwear, anything that would allow them to bring as much as possible to their relatives. Rodolfo was no exception, and all of the family contributed to the large load of gifts he was taking to Cuba.

***

On the day of the flight, the entire family gathered at Miami International Airport: Arturo and Martica, Clara, her husband, and two children, and Lissy and her family. There were hugs, kisses, smiles, and tears. When Rodolfo was walking away, Martica couldn't control herself.

"Come back home, son," she said.

Arturo looked down. Rodolfo turned around and smiled at her.

"Don't worry, Tía Martica," he said. "I'll be back."

Rodolfo then exchanged glances with Lissy, placed his fingers flat against his lips, and threw her a kiss.

Later, as Rodolfo sat on the airplane, the reality of this trip hit him. His mother had not written to him in a while, and he, hoping to surprise her, didn't tell her he was coming. He kept imagining the encounter with his parents, except that he didn't know anything about his father. His mother had not heard from him or his sister in a couple of years.

To relieve tension, he looked at the other passengers, many of them accompanied by families. That's when he noticed that the man sitting next to him appeared familiar. Rodolfo kept looking at him, and when the man did the same,

Chapter 21

Rodolfo would turn his head the other way. That is, until his curiosity won.

"Excuse me, sir," Rodolfo said to the middle-age bald man. "I'm sorry to bother you, but your face is familiar."

"I'm sorry," said the stranger. "I don't think I remember you."

"You sound Cuban," Rodolfo said. "When did you leave Cuba?"

"October 1968," the man said.

"Was that your second attempt at leaving that month?" Rodolfo asked.

The stranger glanced at him, his eyebrows pulled together.

"As a matter of fact, yes. I gave up my seat to a boy the first time I tried to leave."

"Do you remember the boy?" Rodolfo asked.

The stranger smiled with a hint of sarcasm and said, "How can I forget?" And then he started to scratch himself.

"What do you mean?" Rodolfo asked.

"My family and I have spent over ten years apart because of what I did," the stranger said with contemplative eyes.

"What do you mean?"

"Their visas arrived a couple of days after Castro stopped allowing people to leave. Had I left when I was supposed to, we would not be having this conversation."

"You can say that again," Rodolfo said.

"I don't understand," said the stranger. "Do we know each other?"

Rodolfo shook his head. "Look. I'm so sorry this happened to you. I'm very sorry."

Chapter 21

"Why would you be sorry?" The stranger asked. Then he noticed the familiarity with which Rodolfo glanced at him and added, "Wait a minute. Was it *you*?"

"Yes, I'm the boy you helped over ten years ago," he said. "My name is Rodolfo. My mother's name is Ana. Remember her?"

The man nodded. "What are the chances?" he asked scratching his head. He then shook Rodolfo's hand and told him his name was Rio.

"I can't thank you enough for what you did, but I haven't seen my mother for over ten years either," Rodolfo said. "I grew up with my aunt and uncle in Miami; they have been like parents to me."

Rio glanced at a woman and two young children sitting across the aisle, and his eyes then returned to Rodolfo.

"Does your mother know you're coming?" Rio asked.

"I'm surprising her," Rodolfo said. "What about your wife?"

Rio explained that his wife didn't know he was coming either. Rio and Rodolfo remained silent for a while.

Rodolfo thought about the day he left Cuba and how much his life had changed since. He wasn't the same person anymore. Until the moment he realized he had fallen in love with Lissy, he had not looked at the United States like his home. It was just the place where he lived. Havana was home. Its energy, its sadness, its happiness all ran through his veins and gave him his identity. Yet now that he was returning, he wondered what it would be like.

"I have a favor to ask," Rodolfo asked Rio after a while. "Would you mind if my mother and I visited you and your family? I would like to thank your wife in person. It's not every day that one gets the opportunity to thank someone for changing his life."

"That isn't necessary," Rio said, "But if the two of you want to stop by for coffee, that's fine. Where in Havana does she live?"

"Santos Suárez, near the park," he said. "Are you familiar with that area?"

"Today must be a day for coincidences," Rio replied. "My family lives on Zapote 269, between Dureje and Serrano streets. Do you know that area?"

Rodolfo nodded and agreed to visit Rio. Later, when the plane began its descent, Rodolfo felt a knot in his stomach, wondering what he would find. So much could've happened in ten years, and he was about to discover just how much.

After clearing customs, Rodolfo approached the area where families awaited. So many faces stared at him, trying to discover a loved one, yet he felt lonely, realizing that none of those longing gazes were intended for him. Walking through the airport brought back memories of the day he left. His mother was so desperate to get him out of Cuba, and he so unloving towards her when she hugged him. Now, all he wanted was to hug her and thank her for the blessings she had bestowed upon him through her unselfish act.

Rodolfo took a cab home. The warm smile on the driver's face when he helped Rodolfo with the luggage and went out of his way to make him feel welcome made him realize that the driver thought of him as someone bigger than he was. The driver asked him so many questions about the United States, and his eyes sparkled when he listened to Rodolfo.

"You're so lucky," the driver said.

And at that point, Rodolfo didn't know how true those words were. Rodolfo's eyes focused on the city that passed by. Havana held so many memories. He saw women walking around dressed in strapless tops, a pair of shorts, and flip flops; kids playing shirtless on the streets; a combination of new Russian cars and old American cars making their rare appearances, as most people rode on public buses and old bicycles, or walked.

Several tall walls displayed socialist emblems. *"Patria o muerte, venceremos,"* one of the signs said. He chuckled. To Rodolfo, it seemed as if Havana were dying a slow death. There, time stood still while the rest of the world moved forward.

When the driver began to approach Santos Suárez, Rodolfo felt a knot in his stomach. Almost home, he thought, noticing the state of disrepair of the streets and the colonial-style houses along the way, unpainted, dressed with mildew and mold that grew like tree branches. The tropical landscape looked green and lush in some of the blocks, defying the broken streets and unpainted houses. As the sun began to set on the horizon, shirtless children played outside with homemade balls or crushed almonds—picked from almond trees—with rocks, on street corners, like he did when he was a child. A handful of people stood in line at the corner bodega, which seemed so small to him now in comparison to the supermarkets in the United States. The bodegas had several empty shelves, visible from the road. His mother had told him about the meager food quotas that never lasted the entire month. But Cubans remained hopeful, and in their resourcefulness had converted bread sprinkled with salt and oil into a staple food.

Rodolfo asked the driver to stop at the house where he had spent several years of his life. Chills went through his body when he saw it. If he could only knock on the door, and find, not strangers, but his mother and father sitting on the sofa watching television, his sister doing her homework or arguing with her parents about silly things. Oh, how he wished those times could return, even if for a few minutes. But he didn't knock, he just looked at it, reminiscing, imagining what was.

Moments later, the driver left Rodolfo in front of a dilapidated three-story building. People coming in and out stared at him with curiosity as he headed for the stairs. He smiled at them, said hello, and began to carry his heavy load upstairs. He thought about going to his grandmother's apartment first as he passed by it, but he decided to keep going. When he arrived at the number his mother had given him in her letters, he stopped, dropped his luggage on the floor and took a deep breath. Then he closed his eyes for a moment and knocked on the door. Nothing. No one answered. After several knocks, the door of the apartment next to his mother's opened, and a wrinkled, thin woman came out and asked what he wanted.

"My mother lives here," Rodolfo replied. "She isn't expecting me; I wanted to surprise her."

"You don't dress like the people here," the woman said. "Do you live in the United States?"

"Yes, I live in Miami now. I haven't seen my mom in over ten years."

The woman shook her head and took a few steps towards him. "Son, come with me," she said, patting him on his arm. "There's something you need to know."

Without waiting for his reply, she turned around and began walking towards her apartment with uneven steps, her back arched by the weight of her years.

"Is everything okay?" he asked. She ignored him and kept walking, leaving him no option but to follow her.

"Sit down," she said when they entered the dark apartment. "Let me bring you a cup of coffee."

The woman's apartment smelled like mildew and was furnished only with two rocking chairs, a square wooden table, and four chairs. A statue of the Virgin of Charity sat in a corner, surrounded by candles and food offerings.

He placed his bags on the floor and sat in one of the rocking chair while an uncomfortable feeling of tightness grew in his stomach. She returned moments later, walking at a slower pace than before while balancing two steaming cups of coffee in her arthritic fingers. They drank the liquid within seconds. He expected the flavor to be consistent with that of the Cuban coffee he drank every day in Miami, but it didn't taste right. She noticed his expression of dislike.

"I'm sorry about the taste," she said. "People here say that the government is adding grated green peas and other stuff to the coffee... Nothing in Cuba is the way it was."

"It's fine," Rodolfo said. "But... could you tell me what is going on? Where's my mother?"

"There was a woman who lived here for a long time," she said talking with her hands. "I said hello to her sometimes, but she never said much. Then I stopped seeing her for a while. In fact, I thought she had moved."

"And what happened?"

"Well," the woman said. She took a deep breath and then exhaled. "I don't know how to say this," she added.

"Could you tell me what's going on please?" Rodolfo asked with an alarmed expression.

"The woman who lived next door...She's dead."

Rodolfo got off his rocking chair abruptly and shook his head in disbelief.

"I don't understand!" he said, raising his tone of voice. "What do you mean she's dead? What happened?"

"All I know is that I heard people scream," she said, gesturing while she spoke. "I went out to see what was going on. I kept hearing the words 'she's dead; she's dead.' Later, I heard people say that the woman had jumped from a balcony. Neighbors said they had seen her drunk several times, and that, after a while, she looked unrecognizable."

Sitting on the old rocking chair, Rodolfo placed his head between his hands and looked down.

"It can't be! She can't be dead!" he said, choking up.

The old woman approached him with slow steps and touched him on his shoulder.

"It's okay to let your sadness out, son. Don't keep it inside because it will eat you."

With his head bowed and covering his face with his hands, he sobbed for a while. Standing in front of him, she made the Sign of the Cross, placed her bony hands on his head, and closed her eyes.

"It's okay, my child. There's no shame in crying for a mother."

When the tears stopped flowing, he stayed in silence, thinking about her lackluster letters and the slurring of her words during the last few times they had spoken—signs he chose to ignore to convince himself that she would find a way to get better. Angry at himself, he took a deep breath and wiped his face.

"Where is she?" Rodolfo asked.

"I don't know," she said, leaving his side and sitting on a rocking chair. "They may have taken her to the morgue, and who knows what happened when no one claimed the body."

"What do you mean?" he said. "My grand-mother and her sister live here. Their apartment number is 210."

"I'm sorry, but the two older women who lived there moved a long time ago. A young couple lives there now."

Their conversation was interrupted by the abrupt opening of the front door. An old bald man entered, walking a small, thin dog. He had a big belly but thin arms and legs.

"Patricia!" he yelled. "I can't keep walking this dog if we don't give him more food. The last thing he needs is exercise!"

"The exercise is for you, not the dog!" she shouted.

"What?" he asked.

"Ah..." she said, waving her hands in dis-missal. "You're as deaf as a post!"

"Señora, I should go," Rodolfo said. "Thank you for the coffee."

"Who are you? Ziomara's kid?" he yelled.

"Stop yelling!" Patricia shouted. "He can hear you fine. No, he's not Ziomara's kid. Don't you see the way he's dressed?"

"Well, Señora Patricia. I should go now." Rodolfo embraced her. "Thank you for the coffee," he said. Then, reaching into his bag, he took out a small package and handed it to her."

"This is for you," he said. "It will bring some memories of the coffee you used to drink."

Patricia smiled.

"Oh Manolo, look at the pretty bag this young man just gave me."

She held Rodolfo's face with her hands and kissed him on the cheek.

"I hope you find your mom's body soon, son," she said. "And now that I think about it, you should go talk to Carmen, the woman in charge of the CDR. Not much happens here that she doesn't know."

The CDR, or Committees of Defense of the Revolution, were the people in each block appointed by the government to keep an eye on the neighbors and to report any suspicious activity.

Rodolfo took his bags and left to begin the search for his mother. But he also needed to find the whereabouts of the rest of his family. He hoped Carmen would know something.

CHAPTER 22

Carmen lived in one of the better houses in the neighborhood. It had a fresh coat of light-green paint and a pretty garden. In her sixties, the round-faced woman didn't strike him like someone who would be in the role of the neighborhood snitch. She had a kind smile and offered him coffee and cookies. After inviting him to use her telephone to contact his family in Miami, Carmen explained that she knew his grandmother well and was surprised when she and her sister left without telling her anything.

"I will never understand why she left her daughter alone, like Ana's husband had done, especially in the fragile state she was in," Carmen said. "It was her only daughter."

Rodolfo didn't understand why she would have done that either. There had to be a powerful reason for his grandmother to leave just like that.

Rodolfo asked her about the rest of his family. She had not heard anything about Rodolfo's father for a few years. He and his daughter came to visit Rodolfo's grandmother in 1976, and then in 1977, she and her sister moved away.

For months, Ana locked herself in her apartment and had a boy, who Carmen had not seen before, run errands for her. Carmen asked other neighbors about the boy. Someone said he was the son of a woman who had moved to Santos Suárez from the Oriente Province, but the boy was mute and deaf, and would get angry if anyone spoke to him. So she decided to leave him alone. After all, she didn't believe someone like him posed a risk.

Later, Carmen learned Ana had quit her job and assumed that Rodolfo would be sending her money and food. She tried to speak to Ana on a few occasions, but she never opened the door, so Carmen stopped bothering her, hoping time would heal her. After Ana started to leave the apartment again, she looked like a different person. She was thinner and dressed in oversized clothes, with her long black hair covering part of her face. If anyone spoke to her, she ignored them.

"That was not the Ana I remembered," Carmen told him. "But I hear that mental illness can do that to a person."

Carmen and Rodolfo spoke for a while longer, and then she talked to one of the few neighbors who owned a car about taking him back to his hotel.

Two hours before midnight, a private vehicle left Rodolfo in front of the Hotel MarAzul in Santa María del Mar, located on the northeast coast of Havana. Jacinto, the driver, offered to return early in the morning to take him back to Santos Suárez.

When Rodolfo entered the spacious lobby, he noticed the hotel restaurant was closed. However, after registering and talking to the receptionist, a worker prepared him a ham and cheese sandwich with homemade mayonnaise, and brought him a beer. Rodolfo had no desire to eat, but finished everything, since he had not eaten anything all day.

He thought about walking on the beach, located across the street, anticipating the sound of the waves and fresh air would help him clear his thoughts. However, after struggling to stay awake, he went to his room. While walking down a dimly lit corridor, he saw a young, scantily dressed woman an old man. He later learned that prostitutes frequented this hotel and wished he could have stayed somewhere else, but it was too late, as his travel package was all-inclusive and permitted no changes.

The next morning, after breakfast, Jacinto picked him up on his 1955 red Chevrolet. Rodolfo grimaced when he entered the car and noticed its interior smelled like gasoline. He lowered the window.

Assuming that Jacinto had not eaten breakfast, Rodolfo brought him a ham and cheese sandwich and a bottle of mango juice. After the first bite, the tall, thin man of around sixty years of age, said with shining eyes and a broad smile:

"*Coñó!* The good life! Do you know how many years it has been since I ate a sandwich like this?" He waited a moment and when Rodolfo did not guess the answer, he added: "Almost twenty years. Thank you for the sandwich and for allowing me to provide you my humble services. This is an old car, and it doesn't smell good, but I keep it in good condition. I repair it myself."

"The engine sounds good," Rodolfo replied, unable to say anything positive about the car, which had a brown interior with various tears and a cracked dashboard.

Rodolfo could now see the front of the six-story hotel, lined with palm trees and shrubs, of modern and basic construction. Someone at the hotel told him that the Bulgarians had built it. He also noticed the empty streets and desolate surroundings, while Jacinto kept asking him questions about the United States.

The trip to Santos Suárez lasted about thirty minutes. The Havana Rodolfo explored along the way depressed him: the broken streets, unpainted houses, banners with communist emblems everywhere. Even his neighborhood seemed different, haggard and tired, although the green and leafy vegetation and orange flamboyant trees adorning a few blocks, contrasting with the blue skies, gave it life and hope.

Rodolfo began his journey with the house where he'd lived before leaving Cuba. It had the same green paint, now discolored and peeling, and a colonial construction, with high ceilings and round columns on either side of the porch. Jacinto waited outside, in his car, and Rodolfo walked towards the porch. He looked around before knocking on the door, remembering the old times. After a few minutes, a woman in her seventies opened and asked what he wanted. He told her he'd come from the United States and explained who his parents were. After that, she seemed more affectionate, and asked him to come inside.

"Let me bring you a cup of coffee," she said.

"Don't worry, ma'am," said Rodolfo, looking around and noticing the ceilings propped with wood trusses. "I won't be here long."

She sat on a wooden chair and asked him to sit on the sofa, in front of her.

"I came to see if you knew anything about my family. Carmen told me what happened with my mom. This afternoon I'll go to Colón Cemetery to see if anyone can tell me what they did with her body."

Rodolfo stared at the tile floor with a sad expression.

"I'm sorry about your mom. So young and full of life. As for your dad, I know he and your sister moved from here to an apartment in La Habana Vieja, near a cousin of mine. I'll give you the address, but I don't know if they still live there."

"Thank you very much, ma'am."

"Hey, would you like to take a tour of your old house? I know you lived here for several years."

Rodolfo thanked her for her gesture, and she took him from room to room. The house felt smaller than he remembered. He told her how surprised he was to see the old Frigidaire refrigerator, working after so many years.

"It has been repaired many times," she said. Even the glass ceiling lamp, which his grandfather installed, was there, now dirty and dusty, but intact. The house looked humble and organized. In each corner he found a memory from his past, from the tiny kitchen, where his mother prepared delicious meals; to the bathroom, which his little sister took over, when the rest of the family waited outside to use it. Before leaving the house, the lady gave him a piece of paper with an address. Then, as if she remembered something, she asked:

"Do you by any chance remember Susana?"

The name of his first girlfriend made him think of his past.

"Yes, why do you ask?"

"She and your mother talked from time to time. In fact, she and her husband helped her move out of this house. Maybe she knows something."

"Can you give me her address?"

"Yes of course. It's easy to find. She lives in front of Santos Suárez Park."

Rodolfo wrote the address on the piece of paper the woman gave him and said goodbye to her. Then, he asked Jacinto to go back home for a while, as he planned to walk to Santos Suárez Park and then stop at the *bodega* on his way back.

He began to walk down Zapote Street, in the direction of Santos Suárez Park, observing the broken sidewalks and the cracked pavement. The block was quiet, with a handful of people passing by, carrying loaves of bread. The colonial-style houses, and the few buildings among them, had moldy walls from the frequent floods. A small group of people were standing in line at the corner *bodega*, waiting to buy their quota of groceries for the month.

Rodolfo was glad to hear that Susana was married and had kept a good relationship with his mother after he left. Still, he felt a little nervous, thinking about their encounter. When he reached the corner of Santos Suárez Park, he noticed small groups of elderly people talking, some sitting on the benches, others sitting on concrete walls. The park looked abandoned, with leaves covering parts of the lawn.

It was 8:30 a.m. when he arrived at the house, the same one he visited during his courtship with Susana. A few minutes after knocking, a girl, of about four years of age, opened the door, and stared at him without saying anything.

"Is your mom in?" he asked.

The girl shrugged and opened the door wide.

"Lolita, who is it?" A woman asked from the back of the house. When the girl didn't respond, a young woman with long, curly-black hair, dressed in a blue blouse with spaghetti straps, and white shorts, came to the door drying her hands. She looked at Rodolfo as if she didn't know him.

"Good morning. Can I help you?" she asked.

"Are you Susana?" he replied, recognizing her.

When she answered affirmatively, he said:

"I'm Rodolfo."

"Rodolfo? Oh my God, I didn't recognize you. You've changed so much! What brings you here after so long?"

She stared at him open-mouthed for a moment.

"Forgive me for showing up like this. I came to see my mom and learned she was dead, so I wanted to ask you if you knew anything about my family."

Susanna asked him to come in and told the girl to go to her room. Then Rodolfo and Susana sat down, one in front of the other. She offered him a coffee, but he said he had already taken two cups.

"I heard about your mom, and I'm so sorry. I hadn't seen her for several months. I've been so busy with my divorce and my daughters."

"Sorry, I didn't know you were divorced," he said.

She looked at the tile floor and took a deep breath.

"It happened not long ago. He left with another woman, but I'm glad. He never treated me well. He was very violent," she said.

They remained silent for a moment.

"And... are you married?" she asked.

"I found a good woman, like you, and we got married. I'm sorry about your divorce."

"That's life. It's difficult to find a good man, especially the way things are in this country. Men get frustrated, and often women pay the price."

"Maybe you'll find the right man, one who deserves you," he said.

"Like you?"

Rodolfo stretched his fingers.

"I'm sorry I never said a proper goodbye. You deserved it. I also want to thank you for helping my parents when they moved. By the way... where is your other girl? And your mom?"

"My oldest daughter is in school, and my mom met a Spanish tourist, married him, and went to Spain with him. Things have not gone well for her. Well, you can see it by looking at this house. It's practically falling on me. I know that if my mother could, she would help me monetarily."

Rodolfo looked at the wooden trusses sustaining the dining room ceiling and the unpainted walls, and for some reason, he felt guilty, thinking that if he had not left her, her life would not be this miserable.

It was warm inside the house. Susana removed a rubber band from her wrist and used it to bind her hair into a ponytail.

"Look, I brought a few clothes for my mom, and if you don't mind, I'd like to leave them to you. Maybe you can sell what you don't want," he said.

She looked at him.

"I don't want your charity," she said, evading his gaze.

"Don't look at it that way. I don't have any use for those clothes, so I prefer to leave them with you. Do whatever you want with them."

They remained silent for a moment.

"And... do you have pictures of your wife?" she asked.

Chapter 22

"Are you sure you want to see her? I don't want to hurt you."

"A lot of time has passed. It wasn't easy to forget you, but time helps to heal the wounds. We were young, and I loved you very much. You were my first love."

Rodolfo remained serious, and looked at her, without knowing what to answer. Then, he extracted a picture of Lissy from his wallet, taken on the day of the wedding, and handed it to her. She examined it in silence and returned it to him.

"She looks like a princess," she said.

Susana's eyes filled with tears.

"I'm so sorry, Susana, that things ended up as they did. I never meant to hurt you. You know that if I had stayed here, I would've never left you, but, as my Aunt Martica tells me, we come to this world with our destiny."

Rodolfo returned the picture to his wallet.

"And mine is to be abandoned by those I love," she said, and burst into sobs.

Rodolfo rose up from the sofa, walked towards her, and patted her on her back. With tears in her eyes, she too got up and placed her face very close to his, so close, he could feel her breathing.

"I think you'd better go," she said. "About your dad, I can give you his last address. I don't know anything else."

"If you let me, I'll bring you the clothes tomorrow and some money for the girls. Okay?"

She took a deep breath and lowered her head, and Rodolfo gave her a brief hug. Before he left, she handed him a piece of paper with the same address Carmen had given him.

As he walked away from the house, in the direction of the bodega, he felt worse than before. He never thought he would find Susana so defeated and thin, with so much sadness in her eyes.

After a few minutes, he stopped in front of the bodega. Four people stood in line waiting for their turn. Rodolfo noticed several shelves, almost empty, and an old weight on the counter that looked like a metal fountain. When his turn arrived, the attendant, without looking at him, asked him for his ration card. He explained he wasn't there to shop, and told him the purpose of his visit. However, the attendant couldn't give him any additional information.

Rodolfo then decided to go to Jacinto's house and ask him to take him to the cemetery. Cementerio Colón was located about six kilometers from Santos Suárez. Inaugurated in 1871, in the area of El Vedado, it looked more like a historical museum than a cemetery, with tall sculptures and pantheons of various architectural styles, representing different moments of Cuban history.

When crossing the great portico of the main entrance, Rodolfo went to the offices. He explained to an employee the reason for his visit. After going through some papers, the bald and thin man said he didn't know anything about his mother, but then, as if noticing the look of consternation on Rodolfo's face, he decided to make some telephone calls. After a while, the employee told him that Ana had been buried. He couldn't give him any additional information.

As Jacinto drove away from the cemetery en route to Old Havana, he told Rodolfo something that destroyed his hopes of finding the place where his mother was buried.

"Sorry to tell you this, but when they didn't find a family member, it is possible they gave her corpse to some university."

Feeling angry and helpless, Rodolfo looked towards the city. Every additional minute he spent in Havana made him even more detached of the place where he was born. He tried to do everything possible to remove the vision of his dead mother on a table at a university, being examined by a group of students. He wanted to cry and scream. Tears came out, and Jacinto, realizing it, offered him a handkerchief.

They stayed in silence until they came to the front of a haggard building in Old Havana. It was a much poorer neighborhood than Santos Suárez. Small groups of men, in T-shirts, talked on street corners; clothes of various colors hung from clotheslines on several balconies; and rows of unpainted colonial-era buildings stood in moldy attires, some partially destroyed. As in Santo Suárez, the streets were broken.

In front of the three-story building, Rodolfo saw a black boy of about twelve years of age, shirtless and without shoes. He asked him if he knew who lived in the apartment of the number he was carrying.

"My grandmother, my mother, and my brothers live there," said the boy.

Chapter 22

"Are they home?"

"My grandmother is. My mother is out there, working for the tourists."

Rodolfo asked him if he could speak with her. The boy led him to a second-floor apartment, and opened its door. The sound of the hinges made Rodolfo's skin bristle. At that moment, a huge cockroach ran out, and Rodolfo crushed it with his shoe. Sitting on a rocking chair, looking out the window, Rodolfo saw an old woman, her white hair, gathered in a tiny bun behind the nape of her neck. The living room-dining room combo was small, with space for two rocking chairs, and a square table with four chairs.

"*Abuela*, this man wants to see you."

The boy left, leaving Rodolfo with the old woman.

After explaining who she was, she told him that his father and sister had only lived there for a while and, when they moved, didn't say where they were going.

Rodolfo left the apartment and returned to the hotel, disappointed. That night, he fought the urge to tell his wife about the death of his mother. What was the point? Lissy needed to focus on her work, and even if she knew, Rodolfo realized this would accomplish nothing. Then there was Arturo. Rodolfo couldn't tell him over the telephone what his sister had done. The more he thought about it, the more he convinced himself this was a cross he should carry alone.

The next day, Jacinto took Rodolfo to Rio's house. It was then Rodolfo realized that his family lived next to the apartment building where his grandmother and mother had lived. Like other houses in Santos Suárez, it had a colonial-style construction, peeling walls, and crumbling ceilings supported by wooden trusses, but the love radiating from the parents and the children defied the state of disrepair. The boy couldn't leave his father side and looked at him with admiration and pride. The girls laughed while covering their mouths with their hands when their father told them traditional Pepito jokes. After bringing Rodolfo a cup of coffee, Laura, Rio's wife, sat on the sofa next to her husband and the two held hands.

Rodolfo had not yet ruined their night with his troubles. That came a little later, after Rio asked him about his mother. As Rodolfo watched this happy family, the distant past invaded his thoughts. Cuba—he now understood—was no longer his home.

"It is not a particular place we miss; it is the times and the connections we made," his aunt had told him when asked whether she missed Cuba.

He missed those times, before he left Cuba, times that would never return.

When Rio asked Rodolfo about his mother, Rodolfo looked at the children and hesitated. Laura noticed his expression and sent the children to their room. Then, in a low tone of voice, Rodolfo told them what had happened. As he spoke, Laura got off the sofa and placed her arm around Rodolfo's back, like a mother would. She knew about the woman who had jumped off the balcony; but she didn't know where Rodolfo's family was.

Watching Laura's kindness made Rodolfo feel worse. She didn't deserve the time she'd been kept apart from her husband, and all because of him. Their three children, the oldest fourteen, grew up without their father because of Rodolfo. If he could have hit rewind on his life, he would have done so, even if that meant never having the joy of meeting Lissy. She was probably better without him anyway. That was how he felt at that moment. Martica believed that everything happened for a reason, and that statement never made less sense to him than at that moment, as he watched a family that very soon would have to say goodbye again.

Rio told Rodolfo later that night about his plans to stay. He would allow his flight to leave without him.

"Will they allow you to stay?" Rodolfo asked, knowing this would never happen. If Rio attempted to stay, he would be forced to leave sooner or later.

"I don't know unless I try," Rio responded.

Rodolfo never saw Rio or his family again after that night. During the rest of his stay, he dedicated his time to looking for answers. He followed every lead, spoke to every person who knew his mother. But each road came to an abrupt stop, leading him to conclude this was a mystery he would never be able to resolve.

Why did his mother take her life? Why did everyone she loved abandon her?

CHAPTER 23

Worried about Arturo's reaction, Rodolfo asked Lissy to keep the news of Ana's death a secret. Arturo was so desperate to know something about his sister that he asked Martica to call Rodolfo on multiple occasions. Rodolfo was not prepared to talk to him. Therefore, he asked Lissy to tell Martica, via telephone, that everyone was fine, but he was busy working on a critical project, after being out of the office for so many days. Now he had to figure out what to tell his uncle when he asked about the pictures.

Rodolfo felt guilty he'd failed to act when his mother's actions screamed for his help, but he wondered what he could've done to prevent what'd happened, if anything. Sometimes when he came home from work to an empty house, he had outbursts of feelings that shattered him, leaving him depleted of energy. The triggers varied, from the interactions of a family passing by when he stopped at a red light on his way from work to a television commercial. Thinking of the loneliness she must have felt during her last few hours of life devastated him and made him realize how unfair he had been to her at times, and in particular, on the day he left Cuba. If he only had one more chance to tell her how much he loved her, how sorry he was for not being the ideal son.

During his teenage years, she sometimes told him: "Keep ignoring me, son; one day, when I'm gone, you'll regret it." That day had arrived.

"I'm so sorry, Mamá," he said one night, looking towards the sky, overcome with emotions. "You deserved so much better."

Lissy could sense his pain when they had dinner together, and he seemed to be at another place or at night when she returned from the hospital and found him awake staring at the ceiling.

"Does it get better?" he asked her once. "I mean, do you still miss your dad?"

They were lying in bed, Rodolfo on his side with his arm around Lissy's waist.

"When part of you dies, I'm not sure if it ever gets better," she replied. "I keep wondering how it would've been if he had not been killed." She sighed. "Sounds silly, I know, but it helps me focus on the things he would've wanted me to do if he were still here. He used to tell my mom that he wanted his daughter to become a doctor. The day I do, I'll dedicate all of these years of hard work to him." Lissy paused for a moment and caressed his arm lovingly. "What would she want you to do?"

"I think she would want me to find the rest of the family," Rodolfo said, but he didn't know where to start, not if he had to keep his mother's death a secret. He became so desperate he considered going to a fortune teller, like his mother had done when he was in Cuba. For years, Ana kept referring to the accuracy of her predictions. However, when Rodolfo told Lissy about his plan, she asked him if he had lost his mind. Not that he found Lissy's idea much better. She told him he should pray, something he didn't know how to do because in Cuba the government had frowned upon the practice of religion since the early 1960s. Still, he tried mimicking what Martica did when Arturo was in the hospital, unsure if it counted as a proper prayer.

It bothered Rodolfo hiding the truth from Arturo. Since his return from Cuba, Rodolfo had avoided picking up the telephone and going to Arturo's house, but when Martica left him a note in his mailbox inviting him and Lissy to lunch, he realized he had to think of a story.

On the day of the scheduled lunch, when Martica swung the door open to let Rodolfo and Lissy in, Rodolfo noticed that his uncle was not reading or watching television. Instead, he sat on the sofa, observing Rodolfo from the moment he walked in, his chin resting on his thumb, his index finger across his lip. He didn't get up to greet them. It was Lissy who approached him, a wide smile on her face, and gave him a kiss on his cheek. He greeted her with a serious *buenos días*, his eyes giving Rodolfo a hawkish look, making him feel uneasy. Rodolfo walked up to him and shook his hand. "Hola, Tío," Rodolfo said, but Arturo just stared at him.

As if noticing the exchange, Martica asked Lissy to accompany her to the kitchen. This way,

Chapter 23

Arturo and Rodolfo would have time to catch up, she said. After the women disappeared toward the back of the house, Arturo sprang into action.

"So, did you bring me any pictures from Cuba?" Arturo asked.

"I'm glad you reminded me," Rodolfo said nervously. "I left your camera at home."

"You haven't answered my question," Arturo replied and crossed his arms. "Look, you think that old and stupid are the synonyms. Tell me what's going on. I know you've been avoiding me."

Rodolfo shook his head. "It's not like that, Tío," Rodolfo said scratching his head.

"Something happened to my sister, didn't it?" Arturo said, staring at Rodolfo. "You don't even pick up the telephone when Martica calls your house. And I know you're there. What's going on?"

Rodolfo took a deep breath before responding.

"I didn't find her, Tío. I didn't find anyone. They left the neighborhood, and not even the lady from the CDR knows anything," Rodolfo responded, speaking at a fast pace and with conviction.

"That doesn't make any sense!" Arturo said, getting off the sofa and waving his arms.

"I know, Tío Arturo. I have to do something. I was thinking that if I called Voice of America radio, a listener who might know where they are could get a message to them."

Arturo shook his head and sat down again. He rubbed his face, a look of concern transforming his expression.

"Do you think they were taken to jail?" Arturo asked.

"No, Tío, the woman from the CDR would've told me."

"And you believe the woman from the CDR?" Arturo asked, looking at Rodolfo with a puzzled look. "I can't believe you talked to her. What do you think, that a communist would tell you the truth? Those people would report their own mothers if they could."

"Carmen seemed to me like a decent woman," Rodolfo said.

"Don't tell me you went to Cuba to make friends with a communist," Arturo said, raising his voice and speaking with his hands. Then, pointing at Rodolfo, he added, "Listen to me and listen to me good! If those sons of bitches did something to my sister, I'll go there myself and—"

Arturo stopped talking when he noticed that Lissy had entered the room.

"How are you gentlemen doing?" she asked. Then glancing at Rodolfo, she added: "Is everything okay?"

Rodolfo glanced at her.

"Yes, I was just explaining that I couldn't find my relatives when I went to Cuba."

Lissy remained silent, unaware that *this* would be the explanation that Rodolfo had invented.

"What I can't understand is why Lissy told Martica they were fine," said Arturo.

"I didn't want to worry you, Arturo," Lissy said, forcing a smile. Then in a reassuring voice, she added, "I'm sure they're fine. Don't worry. We'll find them."

Arturo turned his attention toward Rodolfo again, his eyes trying to decipher what his nephew was thinking.

"I'll call Voice of America," Rodolfo said with a calm voice. "It's too soon to worry."

Rodolfo delivered on his promise to his uncle, but when after a few days, his telephone didn't ring with news from Cuba, he began to lose hope. He wanted to return to Cuba, thinking that perhaps by then, someone may have heard something. Lissy persuaded him to wait until she finished her residency at Jackson Memorial Hospital. She would accompany him.

Upon completing her residency, a local physician group hired her, and the couple began to plan their trip to Cuba.

***

Martica was preparing breakfast in the kitchen while Arturo read in the bedroom when the bell rang. It was only eight, too early for visits. Curious and concerned, she dashed to the door and peeked out. The familiar face made her smile.

"What a surprise!" Martica said, swinging her door open and kissing her daughter on the cheek. Clara had come unaccompanied. By this time, she and her family had moved to Kendall, a suburban neighborhood of Miami, and she didn't visit as often as prior to having her second baby.

Clara sat on the sofa and was about to say something to her mother when Martica rushed to the kitchen, rambling something her daughter couldn't understand. Clara was so desperate to tell her what was going on, that she considered following her into the kitchen. Instead, she looked around the room, focusing on her parents' colorized wedding picture on the wall, taken before Castro came to power. Her mother looked beautiful, with her long brown hair in curls adorned by miniature flowers and eyes that looked like the ocean. Arturo had combed back his dark hair and wore an elegant dark suit that made him look strikingly handsome.

The passage of years erases everything, she thought.

Martica reappeared moments later with two steaming cups of coffee.

"Now we can talk," Martica said, handing one of the cups to her daughter. Clara drank it fast and placed the empty cup on the coffee table.

"I'm sorry I came this early, Mom, but the news I bring you can't wait," she said, rubbing her hands together with a happy expression. "I could've called, but I wanted to see your face when I tell you."

"That's a long drive just to see my face, so this better be good," said Martica. "Is everything okay?"

"You'll be shocked!" Clara said. "I know I was, and I don't get shocked easily."

Sitting in a rocking chair across from her daughter, Martica placed her hand on her chest.

"Ay Clarita, you're worrying me," she replied. "What happened? You're not pregnant again, are you?"

"No, Mom. I'm not pregnant. And no, you don't need to worry," she said. "I'm the bearer of good news." Clara smiled from ear to ear, unable to contain her excitement. "I wanted to be the first one to tell you because I know your friends. I'm surprised your phone is not ringing already."

"Tell me what? Please say it once and for all!"

"It's about Dad's sister Ana and her family."

"What about them? Do you know where they are?"

Clara smiled and did a happy dance from her seat.

"Mija, just tell me!" Martica said.

Clara pressed her hands together and moved joyfully on her seat. "They were on the radio looking for Dad and Rodolfo!"

"You mean, on the Voice of America radio station?"

"No! They were on a local radio station. They're in Miami!"

Martica raised her eyebrows in surprise and gave her daughter a perplexed look.

"But how did they get here? I don't understand," Martica said.

"And you think I had the patience to wait for them to tell me? No, Mami. I wrote down the phone number and got dressed. Simon stayed with the kids."

"Oh, Clarita. You don't know how happy you make me," said Martica, wiping a tear. "Arturo won't believe it!"

"Well, are we going to tell him now?"

"This is too much for him. I prefer to take my time."

"Tell me what?" Arturo asked, having listened to a portion of their conversation.

With her eyes, Martica begged Clara not to tell him. Clara rose from the sofa and kissed her father on the cheek. Then father and daughter sat next to each other.

"Well," Arturo said looking at Clara. "I'm waiting."

"Let me bring you a glass of water first," said Martica. "This is good news, but I want you to be prepared. I'll be right back. Clarita, don't tell him, okay?"

She smiled. "My lips are sealed, Mom."

Arturo shook his head. "The two of you are always making a big deal about everything," he said as Martica walked away without paying attention to him. "Clarita, I keep telling your mother that I'm strong as an ox, and she doesn't believe me."

Clarita giggled. "Yes, Dad. We believe you. All I know is that you're gonna be so happy when you find out."

"Just tell me!"

"Nope!"

Moments later, Martica returned with a glass of iced water. Arturo drank less than half and placed the glass on the coffee table.

"Happy?"

"Yes. Well...," said Martica calmly. "It's about your sister. She's fine. Everyone is fine."

"How do you know? Where's she?"

Chapter 23

"My love, your sister and her family are in Miami."

Arturo studied his wife's face with a puzzled expression. "Martica, are you playing with me? If you loved me, you wouldn't play like this, chica." His mortified look stiffened as he glanced at his wife then at Clara.

"I heard Ana on the radio this morning, Dad. She's looking for you and Rodolfo. I have her phone number."

Clarita took a folded piece of paper out of her purse and gave it to her father. He unfolded it and looked at it in disbelief. "But how? How did they get here?"

"We don't have the details. That's all we know," replied Clara.

"I don't know what kind of joke this is, but it's not good to play with people's feelings like this," Arturo said, looking at the telephone number again.

"My love, it's no joke. Do you want me to call her?" asked Martica.

"No, I will," said Arturo.

"Let's wait about an hour," Clara suggested. "She may still be at the radio station."

"What radio station?" Arturo asked.

"Dad, are you thinking—"

"Yes. Let me get dressed. Please look up the address in the yellow pages and take the Atlas. I still get lost in this town."

Clara offered to drive her parents, as she knew where the station was and her father was in no condition to drive. Martica sat next to her daughter, and Arturo in the back seat. Clara could sense his nervousness from the way his eyes wandered outside the window, as if the once familiar streets all of a sudden appeared unrecognizable. He massaged his temple when he thought no one was looking.

When they arrived, Clara parked her white '78 Monte Carlo near the entrance. They had just gotten out of the car when the front door of the station opened. A woman and a man seemingly in their early fifties, accompanied by a young lady, began to walk towards them. Arturo's eyes focused on the older female: long black hair, up in a ponytail, thinner than he remembered. As she came closer, he noticed the lines in her face drawn from the corner of her eyes, and a premature groove below her bony cheeks. She wore someone else's clothes, a white t-shirt and jeans—big and baggy on her—and white tennis shoes that had seen better days. Not the sister he remembered, wearing pretty dresses and heels since she was twelve.

"Ana?" he said, recognizing her eyes. He couldn't forget those eyes, so full of emotion on the day he had left.

She stopped for a moment and stared at him.

"Arturo?" She dropped her purse on the ground and ran to him. "Oh my God, my brother! I can't believe it. I can't believe it's you."

She threw herself in his arms and they embraced; almost twenty years of suspended hugs brought tears to the eyes of those who witnessed their encounter. They cried for a while in each other's arms, and she kissed his cheeks a dozen times and he hers, while she repeated, "My brother, my big brother. Thank you, God, thank you."

Martica and Clara had never seen Arturo so vulnerable, so expressive—not even when he lost his son. Back then, his emotions took refuge inside, but now, it was as if a pressure relief valve had been removed, and he emanated happiness from every pore, a happiness he needed to feel human again.

After more family hugs and reintroductions, Ana, Sergio, and their daughter Amanda, along with Clara and her parents, squeezed into Arturo's car. On the way, Clara began to plan the great surprise she was going to give Rodolfo.

It was Saturday, and Rodolfo and Lissy were home. When he picked up the telephone, and Clara told him she had a surprise for him, he asked what it was. She did what she always did. "I'm not telling you! It's a big surprise, so get ready and bring Lissy."

While Arturo's family waited for Rodolfo, Arturo filled Ana with questions. Ana explained that her husband had built a boat with stolen materials, risking his life in the process. Anything could've happened if the authorities found out. Ana and Sergio had been apart for years after she turned to alcohol as an escape.

"I did things, my brother, I should've never done," she said holding her husband's hand and looking down in shame. "My family was all I had. I was desperate. I deserve what my life became, every bit of it. But I'm glad that this man came to my rescue when I needed it the most, when I was about to be lost forever."

With eyes full of tears, Ana squeezed Sergio's hand, and he smiled at her with lips pressed together. He too had changed. He now had a full head of grey hair and deep wrinkles around his tanned face. His rough hands revealed several bulging veins. Their daughter Amanda sat by her mother, all grown up and beautiful like her mother had been in her younger years.

The sound of the bell interrupted the family's animated conversation. Clara dashed to the door, and the moment she opened it, and let Rodolfo and Lissy in, Rodolfo felt as if he had stepped into a different reality. There, in front of him, the ghost of his mother had taken human form. How could it be? How could she be alive? He had cried for her. He had to climb out of the mountain of guilt to become himself again. Ana ran to him and embraced him, but he was still in a haze, unable to understand. Lissy stepped aside, wiping the tears that had rolled down her face.

"I thought you had died," Rodolfo said in a faint voice as his mother kissed him and hugged him. All eyes turned to him.

"You thought she was dead?" Arturo asked.

Ana set him free and caressed his face. "I don't understand," he said.

"I went to your apartment," Rodolfo said, looking at his mother with a confused expression. "The neighbor next door said you had jumped off the building. I tried to find where they had taken you, but by the time I did it was too late. When no one claimed the body, they buried you."

"Oh no!" Ana said placing her hands over her head. "That poor woman!"

Ana didn't have a chance to elaborate because at that moment, Rodolfo's father, who had been waiting to greet his son, extended his hand toward Rodolfo to shake it, like he would with a stranger. Rodolfo smiled and opened his arms.

"Come on, Dad," Rodolfo said. "Give me a hug. I missed you, Viejo."

They embraced, their laughter mixed with their tears. Sergio then patted his son on his shoulder. Sergio looked thinner than when Rodolfo left Cuba, with sunken eyes, edged by dark bags.

"You look like an important man, son," Sergio said. "I couldn't... recognize you."

"What about me, brother?" Amanda asked waving her hands. "No hugs for your little sister?"

Rodolfo embraced his sister, and their parents joined them in a long and emotional family hug. Arturo and Martica exchanged glances, then looked down.

"Mom, Dad," Rodolfo said, noticing the sadness that had overcome Martica and Arturo. "There's something important I need to tell you. First, I want to introduce you to my wife, Lissy, the love of my life, my friend since I arrived here."

Rodolfo's parents and Amanda greeted Lissy with kisses and hugs.

Then looking at Arturo and Martica, Rodolfo added: "Mom and Dad, I also want you to know that during all the years we were kept apart, I wasn't alone. Arturo and Martica were my parents. So, I feel fortunate that today I have two sets of parents."

Martica and Arturo tried to contain their tears.

"Okay, okay," said Arturo. "Enough with all this crying and woman-stuff. This family is going to take control of all these emotions. Let me take everyone to Versailles for lunch! We have a lot to celebrate."

Clara opened her mouth wide. "But Dad, you always said that restaurants are a waste of money."

"Did I ask you for your opinion?" Arturo said, crossing his arms and looking at his daughter with a defiant but playful look.

"Wait a minute!" Rodolfo said. "I'll be the one paying for everyone's lunch. That's the least I can do for my two sets of parents and my two sisters. Besides, we have other reasons to celebrate. We wanted to wait a little longer to make the announcement, but what better time than this?"

Martica shook her head.

"So what is it now? What other secret are you hiding from us?" asked Martica.

"Let's put it this way," Rodolfo said. "In a few months, Clara will not be the only person in our family who has children." His statement was followed with more hugs, laughter, and tears.

It wasn't until later, when they were waiting for the food, that the family heard the story of the woman who lived at Ana's apartment. She had been running away from an abusive husband and needed a place to stay, while Ana wanted someone who resembled her to stay in her apartment. The woman, Elizabeth, moved in in the middle of the night. She colored her hair black, like Ana, and kept some of her clothes, as well as money and most of the food Rodolfo had sent. Leaving someone behind who looked like her allowed Ana to disappear from the neighborhood without raising suspicion. Ana then joined her husband, who by that time had the boat ready for the journey.

"I knew she was a troubled woman," Ana said. "But I didn't think she would do that."

Martica crossed her arms and stared at Rodolfo.

"I'll never forgive you, Rodolfo, for not telling me that your mother was dead. Never! You hear me?" Not having a mean bone in her body, Martica sounded more comical than angry.

Clara laughed. "But Mom, she wasn't dead!" she said.

"That poor child, enduring his mother's death alone. It's unforgivable that you didn't tell me, Rodolfo. Why is this family always keeping secrets?"

Everyone laughed, except Arturo, who rolled his eyes.

Ana proceeded to tell her family about the treacherous journey. Sergio had used a motor from a 1952 Chevrolet pickup truck and a propeller that allowed the boat to travel at no more than 8 mph. Bringing enough food for a couple of days—two loaves of bread, a few cans of condensed milk cooked in the pressure cooker, two jars of peanut butter that Rodolfo had sent them, chamomile tea, and as much water as they could fit in the small boat—they left the northern coast of Havana under the cover of night, afraid they would be caught by the Cuban authorities and sent to jail. After the first two hours, when the lights of Havana had already faded, Sergio calculated that the risk of being caught had passed. Yet a new danger emerged. The Florida Straights had claimed the lives of thousands of people, and they knew what could happen, from shark attacks to changes in weather, that could instantly convert their boat into a death trap.

Three hours after they left Cuba, before dawn, the winds increased and the sea became choppier, causing Amanda and Ana to get sick. After drinking several sips of chamomile tea and eating a few pieces of bread, they began to feel better. It would not be until much later when their worst fears materialized. By then, over twelve hours had passed since they left Cuba and the first glimpses of the Florida Keys had become visible. They were smiling and hugging each other as a white bird flew above them, when the engine stopped. Having lost one of the oars in the rough waters, Sergio tried to use the other, but when it became evident that he was not making progress, he stopped and fear and preoccupation took hold of them. Realizing they were too far from shore to swim, they had no option but to wait. "The two hours we were stranded were the worst," Ana said.

When a fishing boat later rescued them and brought them to shore, Ana thought that God had answered her prayers.

The arrival of two male servers carrying the food interrupted their conversation. As they began to eat the black beans, white rice, sweet fried plantains, and pork, the dialogue turned to a lighter subject where the future took center stage. To finish off the meal, Rodolfo ordered flans for everyone.

Later that afternoon, Rodolfo learned that his grandmother and her sister had no plans of leaving Cuba. Before the two of them left Havana to move with family to the Province of Camagüey, they embraced Ana one last time, realizing that they would not see her again. They would die in Cuba, like their predecessors. Someone had to care for the dead. That was what his grandmother told Ana.

Ana said little about her past. She wanted to forget Cuba and start anew, and now, more than ever, she valued her husband. She owed him her life and would spend whatever time she had left doing everything possible to make him happy. He had grown more assertive over the years. Still a simple man, he would come to the realization that someone with his talent could do very well making kitchen cabinets in Miami, and it didn't take long for his business to take off.

Amanda started to take classes at the community college and helped her parents with their business. After the exodus of Mariel in 1980, she met a Cuban refugee who knew construction and married him.

Meanwhile, Rodolfo and Lissy had three children, two girls and a boy.

Chapter 23

Everyone in the family committed to each other to stay in Miami. Miami had opened her arms to them when they had nothing. Miami had brought them together.

After all of Rodolfo's children were of school age, Martica drifted away in her sleep. She had always been so worried about Arturo dying before she did that she neglected her own health. Arturo never expected that to happen, and on the day of her funeral, he promised her, as he stood over her open casket, that he would join her soon. A few months later, before he took his last breath, he told Rodolfo, while sitting in front of his television set with the volume muted: "Home is not where we're born, but the place where our dreams come true." By then, Arturo had removed all the pictures of Havana from the Cuba Room and given them away. He replaced them with pictures of Martica, arranged in chronological order, from her younger years when he met her in Havana until the end. The last one, that included Martica and her entire family, had been taken during her final birthday celebration at Arturo's home. As her birthday present, Clara had accompanied her mother to a beauty parlor, where Clara convinced her to color her hair blond. "Come on, Mami, do it for Papi," she told her. On the picture, Martica sat next to Arturo, her face touching his, her blond hair giving her back a few years. She was glowing with happiness.

It was in the Cuba Room, surrounded by pictures of Martica and their son, where Arturo slept after she died. It was there he took his last breath.

EPILOGUE

Several years have passed since Rodolfo reunited with his parents. Now, on Rodolfo's fortieth birthday, a little heavier and wiser than when he married Lissy, he understands the wisdom of his uncle's words. On this cool October night, Rodolfo is watching the news, and images of the Gulf War march by, from rolling tanks to the burning desert. After a long day at her practice, Lissy is in the kitchen with their three kids, placing candles on his cake, thinking he didn't see it when she dashed by the living room on her way to the kitchen.

As he waits for his small celebration, a prequel to the lunch at the Versailles Restaurant on Saturday with the couple's extended family, Rodolfo realizes one simple truth: Since the day he met the awkward girl with geeky eyeglasses in his Algebra class, *she* had been guiding him home.

CREDITS AND ACKNOWLEDGEMENTS

I would like to thank all of the following people for their incredible help in assembling the information that would form the basis of this novel, or for reading and telling others about my books:

My mother, Milagros, for dedicating her life to her family, and for the hours she spent with me, after her cancer diagnosis, telling me about her life during the years the Cuban government kept us apart from my father.

Maria Fernandez, for the hours spent on the telephone, providing information about relevant historical events.

My husband and friend, Ivan, for his patience and support throughout the writing of this book and his invaluable suggestions regarding key sections of the manuscript. To my son Ivan and his wife Gloria for all their support.

Kayrene Smither, a reader and friend who offered to read my unedited draft and always has excellent recommendations. I am so grateful for her friendship and feedback.

My wonderful friends and readers, Jackie Challarca, Mary Trevino, Randall Burger, Yemile Cruz-Hernandez, Jeanie Carlson-Ferraris, Odette Figueruelo, Cary Pérez Waulk, Patricia Ford Gonzalez, Allen Luo, Cecilia Martin, Jackie Challarca, Tyler Schmidt, Ruth Padgett MacAnlis, Miriam Acosta, Clarissa Lima, Patsy Sanchez, Jose Alejandro, and so many other friends from my Facebook page who share my posts and provide me with their opinions.

Credits and Acknowledgements

My mentor, Professor John Fleming (University of South Florida Creative Writing program) to whom I am indebted.

Madeline Viamontes, for answering questions about life in Cuba prior to and after Castro's revolution, and for cooking lunch every weekend during the final months of the writing of this book. Also for helping me with the translation into Spanish.

My sister, Lissette, and my brother, René, (and their children) for their encouragement and for telling people about my books. Also to Jeff, my sister's husband, for all his support.

Our dear Alfredo, who passed away a few days before the publication of this novel. To the beautiful family he left behind. Thank you for supporting me during my journey as an author.

All of my extended family, too numerous to mention, and to people who, although not blood relatives, have become family. Tracey O'Neil, my other sister, thank you!

My growing number of readers around the world, and to the book clubs that have selected my books. Thank you for supporting independent authors.

Kimberly Ruiz, author of the wonderful children's book *The Magic Glove* and her husband Rico Ruiz, for their suggestions on the cover.

Gabriel Cartaya, editor for La Gaceta Newspaper, editor of the Spanish version of my books, professor, mentor, and friend, for all the valuable input in the Spanish version that I have incorporated into the English version of this book. Also, Margarita Polo, author, mentor, and friend.

The wonderful Facebook group Women Reading Great Books for helping me decide which cover was the best.

Credits and Acknowledgements

The History Channel, for the videos and footage about President Nixon and the Vietnam War, including the following articles:

(https://www.history.com/topics/us-presidents/nixons-farewell-video)

(https://www.history.com/this-day-in-history/nixon-declares-vietnam-war-is-ending)

The New York Times, for this very valuable article (no longer available as of the printing of this book).

(https://www.nytimes.com/1976/11/15/archives/carter-with-a-long-list-of-campaign-promises-now-faces-the-problem.html)

Time Magazine, for the June 15, 2015 article written by Lily Rothman, which provided me with valuable information regarding President Nixon's resignation speech.

(https://www.google.com/amp/amp.timeinc.net/time/3919625/richard-nixon-resignation)

NPR for the insightful November 19, 2011 article "Children of Cuba Remember Their Flight to America."

ABOUT THE AUTHOR

Betty Viamontes was born in Havana, Cuba. When she was fifteen years old, she and her family boarded a shrimp boat off the coast of Havana during what became known as the Mariel boat lift. Over two hundred refugees accompanied her that stormy night when many people perished on similar overloaded boats. Since the family arrived in Key West in 1980, Betty's mother told everyone: "One day, my daughter will write our story." Betty's parents have passed away, but in 2015, Betty fulfilled a promise she made to her mother by publishing the novel **Waiting on Zapote Street,** based on the story of her family. Her novel was selected by the Gulf Coast Chapter of a United Nations book club for its February 2016 reading and has been presented at a local university due to its historical relevance. One of its chapters appeared in the 2016 USF literary journal *The Mailer Review.* Her short stories and poems have been published in literary magazines, anthologies, and newspapers. She is a speaker and holds graduate degrees in business administration and accounting from the University of

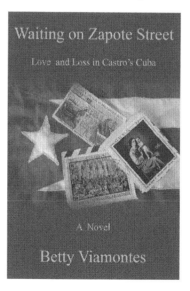

About the Author

South Florida, from where she also received a Graduate Certificate in Creative Writing. She published the anthology *Candela's Secrets and Other Havana Stories* and the novel *The Dance of the Rose*, a sequel to Waiting on Zapote Street.

In 2018, *Waiting on Zapote Street* was a winner at the Latino Books Into Movies Award, Drama TV Series category, an award chaired by the talented actor Edward James Olmos.

About the Author

What are people saying about Waiting on Zapote Street?

From its opening shocks of loss and separation to its thrilling and emotional conclusion, Waiting on Zapote Street gives us a front-row experience of a Cuban family's hardship, love, and enduring love. John Henry Fleming, author

This touching narrative depicts the harrowing trials, loss and separation that hit one particular family in Cuba when Castro comes to power...The author demonstrates numerous layers of Cuban life and belief... Judge, 25th Annual Writer's Digest Self-Public Book Awards

We were captivated by this intimate portrayal of the impact of la revolución. United Nations (UN) Women Book Club of Gulf Coast

The story will take the reader on a rollercoaster ride filled with love and also anger that will test your emotions... It is definitely one of the best books I've read. The Latino Author

Made in the USA
Columbia, SC
20 August 2019